THE CHIAROSCURO

a novel by S. Dinkins

VOLUME 1

The Chiaroscuro: Volume 1
By S. Dinkins

Published by S. Dinkins
Baltimore, Maryland, USA

Contact publisher for bulk orders and permission requests.

Cover design by John Dimes
Book interior design by S. Dinkins
Self-publishing Mentor and book interior formatting by Leesa Ellis of 3 ferns books ➤➤
www.3fernsbooks.com

Printed in the United States of America.

ISBN: 979-8-9884769-0-0

AUGUR

For my dear friend, Tyma-

the keys

-Jerome 1971

Foreword

We were in the public library that morning Jerome and I struck up the dialog which proved to be one of the most consequential of my life. (I was skipping a miserable day of high school, and he was skipping a miserable day at his job.) He'd just recently arrived from the west coast.

We were both pretty young (although I was much younger), and yet, our talk was weighty — like, was "life" even worth the fight, how to survive at the keen edge of madness, how to love without losing, and writing, writing, writing.

As my illiberal parents forbade me to 'see' him, we were stuck just being pen pals, but with so much of that "life" to manage and so many 'jungles' to machete, our correspondence eventually lapsed.

Even so, I never forgot him, and these many years later (through the magic of Aquarian Age technology) I was able to find and reconnect with my old pal. I asked him to tell me how things turned out for him, to write to me like he used to — and he gifted me with a narrative gleaned from the journals he always kept meticulously, in a story which told me everything (ever-entertainingly) in his cleverly iconoclastic, inimitable style.

Maybe there are others who'll also delight in it; I sincerely hope that this finds them.

——Tyma

PART I

THE CHIAROSCURO

WEATHER

A blank canvas

original, primitive, and rough

upon it

I sketch endurance

in light and shade

-Jerome 1972

Eye-catching October spellbound me as always, with her annual cornucopian succulence.

I had admired, as she flung aside fire-hued, flirty intimates high in the trees and reposed her ripened body — but I was smitten when she threw wide those spectacular autumnal legs.... that seductive summons to savor rich harvest and lose myself amidst redolent leaves.

October was tonic, but she has flown.

Austere November now readies her own bleak sojourn — banishing all blue from the sky and spreading a barren mantle over the ground. With cold, numbing fingers she strips October's bright frillies from the hapless trees, as her desolate keening evinces the dolor she wholly intends to share.

It's winter on Welter Street in 1971, when this next chapter begins.

Thursday November 13

    The landlady assured me I would enjoy my new apartment here at
20½ North Welter Street and expressed her pleasure that I seemed
to be 'already making myself at home' (for she noted I'd immediately
shed my mackinaw and long scarf in the sultry living room).

    That radiator in there was *cranking*, but I was so moved by Ms.
Landlady's efforts to "get everything nice and warm" for me, I just
gave her a nod of agreement. Besides, it was so hawkish outdoors,
I'd have welcomed *any* escape from those aggressive elements.

    A ghostly twilight haunted the sky, evoking a potent image from
a long-ago November: me — transfixed and terrified by the advance
of the "evening", as I boyishly pondered its spectral semidarkness
from the window of my grandmother's cozy kitchen. Me — safely back
home at last, having managed to endure yet another lusterless day
in grade school.

    Despite a blackish unease begat by the creepy psychic imprint,
I accomplished a composed countenance as I thanked Ms. Landlady
and went poking about the place....so anxious for her departure,
and the subsequent resumption of my pensive wintry solitude.

    Deeply-charitable-vexingly-voluble Ms. L finally hiked, but not
before again vowing I'd enjoy this comfily furnished 2nd floor flat
and its "extra-special 'plus'" (a thing I pray I will never use):
the small black and white tv a previous occupant abandoned. Then,
she reminded me at least thrice more, to please let her know if I
found that I needed anything else at all.

    I couldn't help but wonder why she'd be so well-disposed and
amicable toward me, and I decided that (since she did seem a little
old-fashioned) perhaps she wasn't hip to the fact that these days,
being sweet with renters is no longer required....or even halfway
expected.

    Maybe, though, I simply reminded her of a grandson of her own.

Friday November 14

    As I stepped out onto the iron fire escape, I faced the wind's razor-edged tantrum — but right behind me, the margarine glow diffusing through the kitchen door's thin curtains, was a reminder that there was warm security readily at hand.

    In the dismal alley behind 20½ North Welter Street, a group of children at play took no notice of me watching from my 2nd floor station. The hostile wind snatched away the sounds of their shouts as sticks became guns in their imaginative hands, and galvanized trashcans became fortresses. I assumed (and yes, *hoped*) that they lived in that identical ages-old apartment house across the way and not this one.

    Too often I hear "childhood is beautiful", its tender innocence so enviable. To me, that 'beauty' is subjective, and that innocence amounts to unfortunate deception.

    In my experience, one had better understand that sticks are sticks and guns are guns — that trashcans are generally trashy (because, you know, <u>trash</u>), and November's raw wind will cut clear to the bone, no matter how vivid one's imagination.

    The wisest among us, obviously (I suppose), are those who know which of these polarities serves the authentic "Self" the most honestly.

    Returning to the kitchen's yellowy haven, I prize the gas heat that hisses from the burners of its dependable old Hot Point stove (for that capricious radiator out in the living room remains just as silently cold <u>now</u>, as when I left for work early this morning).

Saturday November 15

   Tonight (as I sit again near the trusty stove in the kitchen),
a mound of socks I'm listlessly repairing is on the table before
me. My detached attention meanders.... even ruminating on the
outmoded plaid linoleum under my feet (which, this aimless study
concludes, masks another layer — a drab floral one — that's yet
more dated still).

   I hate the city I lie to myself, since my restive mind demands
to know why I'm not out making the busy Saturday night scene with
my peers — why instead, bored and reclusive, I stay home with my
socks, at 20½ North Welter Street.

   I'm craving 'Life', and while a basement encounter earlier today
smacked suspiciously of 'Death', at least it was not the sort of
death I must presently live. Recalling it, is what next preoccupies
my attention, and my sewing lapses anew.

   (While exploring the 'bowels' of this worn-out walk-up, I was
sizzlingly drawn to a dicey, inebriated imp I chanced upon. Her
squinting, hilarious bids to bullseye a lock with the wrong end of
a door key were a captivating hoot, but that spicy little body was
hot as a slap, so, I offered to help with her 'wrangling'.

   Let's just say that if looks could kill, I'd be one dead-ass
ranch hand.)

   A knock on the door snips my woolgathering, and with [too brief]
a pause, I open it to the tall, handsome man smiling shyly at me.
My hand darts impulsively toward my head in an attempt to subdue
the messy mop of wan curls there, for his raven hair is so lustrous
and he is so groomed, I feel suddenly self-conscious and awkward.

   He asks to borrow a cup of sugar for a cake he's baking, and as
I go fetch it I can see him peeping about my living room like a
nosey lady that drops by her new neighbor's house just to spy. I'm
wondering now if he might even be queer, for in his mannerisms and

phrasing, there seems a distinctly coquettish, diminutive quality that his impressive height, growling timbre, and long, lean fitness don't initially imply.

Thanking me for my sugar, he briefly proffers his hand to me — as a royal might do to have it kissed — and then, swiftly departs before I can respond.

The two of them now at least bestow some amusement — a pair of nebulous, distracting toys for my pettish mind as it suffers in dreary sock-mending purgatory.

Sunday November 16

Record lows, but (*again??*) the kitchen's the only place in here that's warm enough to inhabit. I'm out in the arctic living room (trying to get that fickle radiator to cede its latest moratorium) when a staccato rapping disrupts my concentration. My curiosity (as usual) outrivals all else and compels me to answer the door.

Maybe I think, *it's another of the quirky residents...* but as I turn the knob, I cross my fingers that the girl from the basement has sought me out.

It's the tall queer — and he is alarmingly distraught. He's pressing the side of his face as his voice comes in sobbing gasps: **Amigo!! Please— help me!!!**

Upon forcing his hand away, I find oozing scratches that look pretty painful — perhaps made by animal claws. That they *might*, though, be from human fingernails, inexcusably intrigues me; thus, while gathering antiseptic and a styptic, I plot how I'll inveigle him into divulging details I hope to find entertainingly salacious and juicy. (Instead, his weepy sorrow unnerves me so much, I just end up blurting out artlessly **How in the fuck did you get these???** as we sit down on the sofa, and he whimpers under my swabbing.)

He says his wife abhors him, that when she'd announced she was going to vespers tonight to pray again for his "godless soul", they'd had the venomous argument that resulted in her furious swipe at his face... and then, she'd stormed off to church — taking their two young children in tow.

She called me a dirty faggot he snivels. I manage to stuff a tissue into his clenched fist, and he blots his brimming eyes.

Well, are you a fag? I ask, and instantly regret this; not only is it rude, it prompts another wave of the disconcerting grief.

His answer is that in the recent years, his dalliances with men have accrued, and he can no longer delight his wife. Although the mounting indiscretions are devastating his marriage, they seem, nonetheless, an emergent dictate.

How old ARE you? I gasp, confounded by such [implied] naïveté.

(At barely twenty-one, *I'd* likely be given a pass if I were actually so green as to imagine a man this blatantly effeminate might be able to hold his wife's passions indefinitely...but these are ADULTS. Why in the hell would she marry this poor guy here, when it is *so* very clear he is gay?? He said "recent years"— could both of them really only just <u>now</u> be figuring this out???)

He's twenty-seven, the tale unfolds, and his wife, Carmen, is thirty-one. When he was nineteen and she, twenty-three, each was so besotted with the other's ravishing features, they had defied the many dire warnings from loved ones, and eloped. Adding to the (obvious) recklessness of this act, Carmen was also embroiled in a stressful custody battle with her vindictive ex-husband, Rolando, over the two-year-old daughter they shared.

Celeste and I were bonded at the first sight he sincerely smiles, his eyes shimmering with tears — and goes on to describe how four tempestuous years later, Carmen had brought forth their own son, Ramon....a gorgeous little boy with whom he conversely, has an unhappy, contentious relationship.

I recoil at the sudden exposure to this icky familial rancor and dysfunction, and I'm wishing I had thought to eschew the entire conversation (indeed, this entire regrettable contact) before ever blundering into it. Now that I've heard all these 'juicy, salacious details', I would <u>much</u> prefer that I hadn't.

And what's YOUR name? I quickly pivot, for I see *this*, at least, as a safe question.

Floyd he sniffles, again blotting his eyes, and then, drawing back over his shoulder a silky rope of black hair that I swear, has to be a yard long. I find I am staring... helplessly fascinated by its obsidian flow— undulating so languidly, lapping so lovingly at his hipbones...

You are such a good amigo to help me he says, and, as I keep puzzling over his uncommon accent and parlance, I ask him where he's 'from'.

Saltily, he states that his Nordic mother showed no self-respect by wedding his sire, a black Spaniard. His mother, says he, is less than a whore to lay with an ink-skinned man — and an interloper at that....a man from a long lineage of Moorish invaders....an African intruder.

He claims to despise them both.

At first, his umbrage merely baffles me.

Surely he gets that this uniquely mixed parentage has _got_ to be what's imparting these exotic good-looks: that perfect face sculpt and radiant, caramel skin; those well-shaped full lips, and the most mesmeric eyes I've ever seen — an eerie off-olive with dreamy sable lashes and dramatically dark brows. His remarkable stature, refined bearing, and elegant physique confer _such_ a striking air of noblesse, that the vulgar, incongruent malice catches me completely off-guard.

In a split-second, though, I recover.

Amongst other misdeeds, I've a grave record of confrontational responses to racism's searing triggers, and so, prompted by what has become (for me) an absolute imperative if I'm to retain my liberty, I must scrupulously avoid these combustive situations. I simply cannot afford another funky incident.

Floyd's vile rant has just deeply offended my fiercely-held ethics principles — inciting my infamous ire, and rankling the dangerous reactive nature kept caged-up in sleepless submission. Much like an irked viper, my treacherous temper now abandons its deceptive quiescence and begins coiling lethally.

I decide I probably shouldn't hear any more.

Look I say in a seething but tightly-reined dismissal as I rise, **you're all taken care of. You'd best go home...like, <u>NOW</u>.**

He extends his clasped hands desperately toward me in a panicked entreaty.

<u>NO</u>!!! Oh PLEASE, mi amigo!! I think she will try to KILL me!!! How can I face my little boy??? No puedo no puedo.... OH, PLEASE let me stay here with you — only for tonight??? By the morning she will be calm again, and I will go — I <u>PROMISE</u> this!!

Despite my wrath, his frightened breakdown really shakes me. Its anguished despair rips a staggering gash in my emotions (which weakens me, as my stability and resolve bleed out).

Thus, I am full-on furious with myself when I cannot help saying: ***Okay, OKAY! FUCKING <u>OKAY</u>!!***... and I am livid at having been so traitorously betrayed by this soft-hearted (and *most* unwelcome) generosity of mine.

I *am* comforted in small part, by the fact that I have at least weaponized my gesture with a bristling, tacit warning that he'd better keep a very safe distance — but *what* wayward part of me could have decided I should bring a complete stranger into my home, and much worse, allow him to stay over???

Listen, asshole I sternly admonish this renegade internal element, *you know damn good and well you cannot open this space... ...and PRIVACY is how that gets <u>DONE</u>.*

It's no surprise that the emphatic inner averment would elicit a metallic vibration in my mouth — the odd tingling that so often occurs when I have patently lied.... especially when it's been to <u>ME</u>. I know I'm just lip-serving that "oath to privacy" now, for I will violate it without hesitation if I get a chance to bed down my basement muse.

Floyd, of course, is unaware of the discomforting bind.

He thanks me effusively, and dabs once more at those sublime lashes — now wetly clustered by his tears, into utterly charming, silly-looking stars.

Well I reassure myself (since I find I am staring again), *I've simply decided he's in no shape to go home and try to contend with his wife while she is still so angry. It's not like I'm letting him sleep with ME, so, what's the big deal if I offer him my sofa? Any decent neighbor might well do the same...and should.*

I'm satisfied with this, and we both then take refuge in the hearthlike kitchen as I prepare us an unelaborate dinner.

I find myself (in spite of my initial disinclination) pondering his whirl of complexities. Threaded throughout my musing, is a vaguely persistent hope that the sad welts don't scar him; scarring would be a shame, I have decided, since his princely face is so appealingly perfect — and to that end, I've provided cotton balls and aloe vera... advising him to apply it from time to time.

After our dinner, we gaze vacantly at the bluish light of the chattering television, but neither of us pays it much mind — for I am busy with my suppressed, fevered secrets, while across the room, Floyd sits in his own rather still silence, except for occasionally moaning something in Spanish as he gently daubs his injuries.

The living room's flighty radiator has now decided that this vegetative torpor of ours ought to be very well-steeped... and then, served up absolutely sweltering.

I blame November for this infection of lugubrious lethargy; *she* inflicts this pestilent ennui — one that plays spiteful footsie with despair.

Be gone, November, that our frozen passions might thaw at last, and imbue us with all their dared dreams...

....and may we <u>never</u> again turn to this tiresome little box, whose endless, pesky prattle blathers on and on....and maddeningly on.

Monday November 17

   This gray morning, the demented wind throws another tantrum —
its muttering, maniacal chuckles wedged between frenzied shrieks,
as it rattles noisily against the heroic windows.

   Although I had no real enthusiasm for passing a directionless
day on North Welter Street, I called my boss and said I just didn't
feel well today and wouldn't be able to make it in. His response
was typically brutish: demanding I get myself "well" in a hurry,
with a vicious — *Or else* — if I should fail to show up tomorrow...
and that I had better be on time, <u>too</u>.

   I wondered (even as I knew) why *I* seemed to be the only one he
was so reluctant to cut any slack, and then, sighed as I stood over
my sofa-guest. Floyd looked so serene in slumber there, I honestly
hated waking him (plus, I knew his night was fitful, and I felt
like a heel rousing him, when he'd finally managed to sleep).

   You are very kind — thank you, mi amigo he says over breakfast.

   It's a rustic one, for I'm called by another shadowy diorama
from childhood: I'm seeing my favorite plate (creamy sky-blue),
and it's piled with hot bacon, with buttery toast, and bright eggs
— a special treat from my grandmother to help lift my spirits, on
a brooding leaden morning, just like this one.

   The sentimental tableau, however, leaves me melancholy instead,
and my sadness makes me sour.

   As the wind's psychotic screeching grates the inside my head,
I grow irritable and mean-spirited — shooting covert, critical
glances at Floyd, who (I derisively decide) eats just like a dainty
damsel..... and yet *he* tries so very sweetly to cheer me.

   I try hard to dislike him — seeking refuge behind my stronghold
of unruly anger — but the bulwark just caves, and a slow, stealing
resignation forces me to admit that I find him delightful, and far
lovelier than I dare risking comfort with.

I guess I will need to be getting home, won't I he submits, with a rather cavalier [attempt at] equanimity, as our meal draws to a close.

Probably so I concur just as indifferently, and take a sip of tea. He dips his head slightly — lashes like the lushest fronds shading those strange eyes (which this morning now seem the hue of a stormy green sea).

Today...?

Yes I make clear, and send my attention out through the filmy window — unleashing it to wander over the trashcan fortresses and desolate alley behind our moldering old apartment building.

Floyd I venture at last (deciding to answer a nettlesome itch within me, and to disrupt the burgeoning silence that has arisen between us), *I've helped you, and now, I need <u>you</u> to help <u>me</u>.*

<u>*ANYTHING*</u>, *amigo!* he offers earnestly.

Well I continue, with an all-too-awkward nonchalance, *there's a girl in the basement apartment— do you happen to know her name?*

I wait, as the dense brows knit thoughtfully together.

I don't know her name he tells me after what has seemed an eternity.

Oh I say, and our silence resumes.

Returning home this evening from my dinner at the corner tavern (a dark, packed hole of a place, where the local menagerie convenes to drink daily bread), I overtook a man walking down the street in my same direction. It was very cold, and he kept his hands thrust deep in the pockets of a thick peacoat, yet his balding head was unprotected — except for twin slate-colored runners that hugged it like the shoulders of a road, and then merged into the narrow lane of a long ponytail at his nape.

As I passed him, he looked over at me with eyes bright behind
the black-rimmed rounds of his glasses. An imposing trowel-shaped
forehead (edged by wild, bushy eyebrows) met a thin, hooking nose,
and I swear, he even winked slowly... just like a savvy horned owl.

We nodded to each other in the frosty twilight, and he surprised
me by extending his hand in a greeting. He introduced himself as
Walter Brandt, and asked if I'd like to come up to his place for a
"bit of brandy".

Of course not I immediately thought — and was utterly mystified
as to why **Sure— where do you live?** is what came out of my mouth.

Right here he said, and we climbed the stairs to the rooftop
apartment of 20½ North Welter Street.

Every wall up here is hidden by crammed bookshelves, and a low
sloped ceiling obtrudes. It's unsettling and unpleasant — murky,
confined, and fusty.

I am a poet and a scholar he states with not even an iota of
irony, as I struggle for a way to breathe without inhaling. He
dispenses stiff portions of brandy for each of us, lights up a
cigarette, and settles into the unsightly upholstery of a large,
frayed armchair.

I opined <u>very</u> famously about matters of passion and profundity
he boasts between deep, theatrical drags. **I had quite the silver
tongue you know, and at readings I'd have all the chicks eating
right out of my hand.**

He downs his brandy and reaches for another. **Yeah** he says, **it
was all in the palm of my hand...**

As he helps himself to yet a third pour of hooch, I stare into
the unconsumed quantity in my own uninviting cup, realizing much
too late that this Walter Brandt is a soak — that I will soon
become cripplingly bored and depressed if I cannot get out of here
soon.

What could I have been <u>thinking</u>?! I ask myself.

I guess I'd just been chasing diversion — an engaging dialogue maybe....or a sociable drink? An interesting new acquaintance....? While it had been quite obvious from the beginning that he was considerably older than me, I'd wrongly assumed he would therefore be erudite and wry.

I had definitely not anticipated such a pompous sot... eyes no longer bright behind their wise-owl round lenses, but dulled now by a fog of cheap sauce.

The imperative to escape becomes urgent as I feel ever more cornered by Walter Brandt's oppressive flat and its suffocating fetor of chronic neglect — but before I can find my feet and an excuse to leave, he drains his cup and rises abruptly.

I was a <u>much</u> sought-after young man of <u>endless</u> vitality and high spirits...a MOST splendid lad indeed he announces, to my frozen, embarrassed horror. **ALL the chicks craved my recitals — <u>AND</u> I cut a nifty rug on the dance floor—**

As if to prove this, he begins a flailing boogie around the ugly room, chorusing in a voice way too loud — one desiccated by dust and rust, and so weary from its long journey out of the past into this present, unlivable moment. I feel like I'm reading a bad novel; I WISH I was reading a novel — one I could just quickly close the cover on right now, like any other dreadful pot boiler.

Glimpsing himself in a sorely desilvered full-length mirror (propped in the only corner not blanked by a bookshelf), he stops suddenly to appreciate his image. He preens with his fingertips — vainly stroking the vague contours of a Van Dyke beard....like some stereotypical, hackneyed villain.

Addressing this counterpart in a dramatic manner, he intones: **<u>I</u> AM A POET AND A SCHOLAR.**

Then, to me, he snaps **Go home, Jerome. I want some fucking privacy.**

I do go.... and <u>gladly</u>. My mug of his booze remains on the broad arm of my abandoned chair, reflecting.

I decide that its untouched content symbolizes the prickly poet, and I have forbidden "inTOXICation" by whatever "spirit" it was with which he'd sought to suffuse me.

(Since I <u>am</u> feeling so traumatized by the entire [unnecessary] incident, however, I can't understand why I find myself sorry for him. It seems abundantly clear why he lost all he had.)

The minute I'm home, I sit at the kitchen table and scarf down a whole dish of brownies. They're dry as hell, but it's only their calming chocolate I'm after *anyway* (since for me, it works swiftly when my fraught nerves need <u>immediate</u> narcotizing).

Paradoxically, though, I've deliberately chosen the disquieting dull-pink plate...the one with a disfiguring crack down its center.

Just like <u>me</u> I observe cynically.

Hearing my name in Walter Brandt's mouth has triggered a moody gloom. I've never liked my name (and its shortened form, "Jerry" I find even more objectionable).

I can't recall when I *haven't* wanted a name that fit me better, and sometime during my ghastly childhood I decided upon "Luther". In my [juvenile] mind, it embodied the concentrated intensity that my given one belied (and the ravening carnality that I harbored so secretly). Once I finally got the chance to "BE" who I was, I chose to be Luther — and I ache for this essential expression which I must now once more deny.

I try imagining ways to safely restore the archetype to my psychological palette.

I'm underweight now, but maybe if I work out a little, maybe if I can at least recover some of my natural vigor, *that* will help. My self-seclusion has permitted careless inattention to my "look" and to my hectic mop of sandy ringlets, which (for reasons you know all too well) I continue an obstinate refusal to neaten.

Perhaps, though, if I'd just brush it a few hundred strokes now and then (like Grandmother used to make me do), it might decide to forgo its perversity, and agree to arrange itself more obediently on my head.

I have always hated fussing with my hair.

Floyd will do it for me I decide. *I'll get that fucking sissy to brush my hair.*

I'm still blaming November's frigid bite for why I keep feeling so unbelievably mean.

Tuesday November 18

   As I sit this evening beside the stove in the yellowed kitchen,
I hear stomping, crashing, and a shrill voice overhead. It can't
be Walter Brandt's cringeworthy dancing, since he is in the rooftop
apartment, and two other floors separate us. Someone above me
sounds like they're on a demolition mission.

   My own inner pain lies so fiercely guarded in thick silence, I
find myself envious of whatever loose parameters of self-control
allow this person such outwardly demonstrative, clearly anti-social
behavior. To me, banging around over one's downstairs neighbor
and shattering an evening's stillness, are unforgivable crimes
against humanity.

   Desperate for peace and quiet, I try escaping inwardly — but
I find there looking out at me, a snarling, unlovely old woman,
who scowls disdainfully as she delivers her igneous castigation.

   THIS *is what you have become, Jerome! You are just like the*
drabbest old lady — where are your shawl and your apron?!

   Despite the fact I'm not 'old' <u>or</u> a 'lady' at all, I must agree.
You're exactly right — I really am *like a drab old lady —* Drab
Old Lady Jerome. I attach the bitter label and go on lacerating
myself: *Look at me...losing my* MIND *over that fucking girl, when I*
can't be anything *but this goddamned flattened-out turd.*

   I acknowledge the rest of the scathing indictment, too. A drab
old lady like me *should* be sporting some awful apron and a shawl.
I'm smarting from having to admit such shameful things about myself
to myself... but even more unhappy from having to live them out.

   How the hell is that supposed to be helpful*???* I'm forced to
endure this harrowing refusal to emancipate my imprisoned "Luther",
knowing damn well the caged quintessence will just <u>eat</u> its way out
instead.

(And now, I'm wondering whether to go back and strike out this whole miserable entry. The whining admission — not to mention the presence — of such impotence, thoroughly embarrasses me, and I wish I'd never written it.... but since I'll never be able to forget *anyhow*, I guess I should just let it stand. Nobody else, in any event, is ever going to see this but you — at least, I certainly hope not.)

As long as I'm confessing the un-confessable, I might as well address the fact that I'm getting dangerously lonely, and while part of me demands I accept how much I like Floyd and how much I miss his company, I've no choice but to suppress the wish that he'll show up again at my door... because I know (and you do, too) the set-backs that is certain to cause me.

These admissions make me feel stupid, and feeling stupid makes me lethargic; feeling lethargic makes me feel like a dullard, and the thought of being a dullard horrifies me.

If I was stronger, I could accept these terrible things more courageously — but then, of course, if I wasn't stuck having to be such a dull dipshit, I'd not need to admit how disgustingly dull I'm stuck being.

Wednesday November 19

As I left my apartment for the tavern this evening, I ran smack into a commotion in the stairwell: a [middle-aged] couple stood clashing on the 2nd floor landing.

Despite my presence, they did not bother to stop (but as I think back, I realize it was merely the woman who argued, while the man stood quietly resolute, as though he'd had much practice corralling such strident outbursts).

You stay away from that homo I heard, ***he is just trying to solicit you!! His poor wife must be going through absolute hell with someone like THAT always around those two darling children! I will NOT tolerate you stirring up gossip about us, just because you think you ought to act "polite"!!!***

I passed them and continued down the stairs, confident she was referring to Floyd. On the 1st floor (in the vestibule beside our wall of mailboxes), I found him standing forlornly alone; he had to have heard everything.

Why does she hate me? he frets.

Because you're a fag I think to myself, but what I say is: ***Come on. Go get your coat and I'll buy you dinner, if you want.***

His face blinks brightly with surprise and delight.

He asks me to wait, and returns presently in a shapely dark suede car coat with an ostentatious trim of curling white wool.

Oh, dear god I silently shudder.

Where are we going? he asks.

To the tavern I reply.

__Why does she hate me?__ This time he doesn't fret, but *demands*, and does not touch his steaming bowl of diner-thick chowder.

__I__ like you, Floyd I offer.

No, no, I think everyone hates me except you and my little Celeste. Am I so awful? Why do they all despise me?

I remember his disarming charm, stare at the comely caramel face, the ruddy lips, the spellbinding eyes... and I think *What's not to like??*

I don't know I say honestly, trying to figure out who he means.

Tonight, Louise Ramillo told her husband not to speak to me ever again— I heard her. Why??

It's because you're fucking QUEER I snap at last — lacing my words with acid and finality, and not entirely sure why I've done it.

He stares at me awhile in stunned silence, tears standing in his eyes, and I wonder a little whether the cause of this is the brutality of my delivery, the brutality of my statement, or the brutality of my betrayal of his trust in me. I wonder what else he could've been *expecting* me to say, and why he kept pushing me to say it.

But that is not fair; why should that matter so MUCH to them? It does not make me a monster.

Who the hell does he mean??? If it's Louise Ramillo, why the fuck should he give shit what *she* thinks... unless, of course, she's got *Carmen's* ear...??!

Eat your soup I say.

I want to ask him why he doesn't realize that the contempt in which he holds his own parents is every bit as irrational a hatred. I want to say: *You know, Floyd, what goes around comes right on back around.*

Instead (after a packed, long pause), I say **Just eat your soup**—but a distasteful sin of my own has suddenly left mine bitter.

Our walk home in the darkness terminates at the front door of Floyd's apartment.

I wish you could meet Carmen he says unexpectedly. **My wife is such a beautiful woman! But if she sees you, she will hate you because she will think you are just like me — and I wouldn't want ANYONE to hate you, Amigo.**

Though I smile at him and shrug breezily, my inner conversation does not match.

Too late for that, Floyd I think, for I vividly remember the enmity I held for *myself* as I repaired my socks on a lonely Saturday night in the big city... and the hatred in the glowering response of the girl in the basement.

Much worse, though, I am stinging from the gross unkindness with which I've approached my new friend, for I was certainly taught to be better than that. So much for all my high-minded, fiercely-held ethics principles, which *I* haven't even managed to honor.

"Being miserable is no excuse to be mean, Jerome."

I'm aghast to have only used every outward-facing sociability I offer Floyd, to absolve the spiteful inner thoughts about him that I've been entertaining — thoughts I have had to conjure up in order to circumvent my own profound susceptibility to him.

Another of my grandmother's favorite sayings caroms around in my head like a billiards ball: *"We in glass houses had best be careful about throwing stones, Jerome."*

Then (again *unexpectedly*) Floyd says **I will try to find out the girl's name for you** and with a sweet blush and shy smile, he disappears inside.

I retire to my own apartment — my muddled mind entangled in bewildering cords of thought...and undisciplined fire in my body.

It seems that the only thing I feel certain of right now, is that it was Louise Ramillo stomping around over my head last night.

Thursday November 20

I leap to my feet and dash to the door in response to the gentle knocking I hear. I pull up short, however — gruffly snatching my uncharacteristic giddiness by its proverbial shoulder. *How dare you gush like that* is my stern reprimand, as a warm flush of embarrassment seeps up my neck and onto my face. *Stop it!*

As one might do a misbehaving pet one has just disciplined, I continue to eye myself with a cautious distrust as I open the door a crack and peek out. It isn't Floyd at all; it's Louise Ramillo.

Yes? say I, a little bit stunned (and displeased to find that I am so disappointed).

May I come in?

I open the door wider and step aside, relieved that she appears to take no interest in checking out my living quarters. As she walks by me, I notice her expensively coifed bleached hair and the overcooked look of her skin. I also can't help but notice the demonstrative, hefty set of rocks that crust her left ring finger.

Yes? I wonder again.

My name is Louise...Louise Ramillo — do you recognize me from the stairwell last night?

I nod unsociably.

Well she continues, **that's what I came to talk to you about. My husband and I, we aren't ones to make a scene, and I imagine you must be thinking some terrible things about us—**

No I think to myself, *just YOU*.

I want you to realize what you witnessed last night...well... that was not normal for us.

Oh.

Every couple she submits, ***disagrees with one another from time to time, but that...for George and me...was...well...*** unusual.

She is struggling; she wants me to smile and nod and say I understand, but I refuse.

It seems I'm finally "all-in" on the idea that Floyd is my friend, and since this is so, I feel pressed to avenge him.

I now answer a sadistic prompt — not to scorn Louise Ramillo openly, but to instead, undermine and stymie her (which I intend to accomplish by standing obstinately on *my* side of a barrier of polite, feigned naïveté...a vindictive barrier I've contemptuously constructed and placed between us). I wield my passive resistance in a black-hearted attempt to torment her just as much as I can... all for Floyd, because Floyd is my friend.

Alas, though, my tactic backfires — and to my utter revulsion she slithers into a slime of grotesque 'true confessions'.

George is drifting away from me, from our marriage — I can feel it. I just don't know what to do any more. I — I need love.

What you need I think viciously, *is a sound ass-whipping and a brutal screw.*

I'm still full of fire she continues.

You are full of SHIT my internal dialogue responds.

You see, I need someone...younger she says, giving me an insinuating look. I shrug and smile blandly.

I couldn't care less what you need I think to myself, and wish I had said it out loud.

What's your name? she asks, and I answer ***"Jerome"*** wondering why I did not say Luther. Luther would have told her to eat dung and die.

Jerome, are you afraid of me?

I shake my head 'no', the bland smile still pasted on my lips.

Do you find me attractive...?

I tell her she has interrupted my dinner, and ask her to leave. She says ***Please call me Louise*** but I refuse this also. At last, she turns to depart— but not before suggesting she'd very much like to come see me again.

As I close the door, a wicked rush of November's cold ugliness whooshes past me with a cackle that resounds from her netherworld birthplace.

Friday November 21

   It's none too Luther-like to hover by the door on a Friday night, hoping that Prince Charming will arrive. It really does seem I'm living an all-too-familiar fairy tale.

   Fairy!?! The word lands like a hard kick in my middle.

   I double over like I've been struck, as a well-known scalding flames throughout my gut and roars like black fire in my brain. NO ONE is worth what I'll have to pay for this — no guy or even that damned waif in the basement... but she IS, at least, a fucking *girl,* which will not cost me nearly as dearly.

   The true bullseye of this lights-out rage is Floyd...because he excites me — and I am absolutely furious with him that I want him, for *that* will get me in trouble. I hate that he's even there at all, that I ever fucking met him (OR that blasted girl, goddammit).

   I snatch up the mackinaw, wrap my long scarf around my neck in many loops (like it's the noose I'm wishing it was), and dash out the door — determined to escape swiftly, lest he show up now (and further embroil my already rampageous feelings). I know exactly what is expected of me, and not one stinking bit of it has *anything* to do with <u>MY</u> pleasure.

   At the crowded tavern, I encounter the Van Dyke'd Walter Brandt, who acknowledges me with a nod and motions me to sit beside him at the bar. I wonder if he feels any shame or remorse for his behavior the other night.

   If he does, though, he makes no indication.

   Absently, I follow his pretentious gestures as he explains to me how life has been treating him these past few days... and how he's been treating his life. I notice the unrefined look of his hands, with their stubby tar-stained digits and ragged, untended cuticles. Secretly, I compare them with Floyd's long, elegant fingers and kempt nails — then, maliciously berate myself for thinking of him.

I'm drinking less says the poet with a shrug, and washes down a big bite of bread with a swig from a great big beer mug. ***It's just ale for me right now*** <burp> ***no more of all that hard stuff.***

I'm so grateful when the barmaid apologetically interrupts his monologue to take my order, as I am hoping a nice comfort-meal will help quell the hot misery that yet persists in my stomach. Once she has gone, I rummage my thoughts for something engaging to say that might turn the 'conversation' into more of one.

Are you writing again? I blunder, realizing too late what a knife-edge such an insensitive question must certainly wield for him — for I have decided that his time has clearly long passed, and that he must <u>surely</u> see his present life as the great tragedy it so obviously is.

I am astounded when he doesn't miss a beat before answering ***Maybe not right now, kiddo, but you had better bet I will*** <u>***soon***</u>.

He regards me with cool disdain, his eyes behind the owl-round lenses, almost scornful. I notice then, that despite the fact he reeks like a brewery, I actually see little evidence of inebriation in him tonight.

I'll be great again, you'll fucking see. I bet you think I'm just some sad old loser sliding on down the mountain, but baby, I'm WALTER BRANDT. I do what I want, when I want to, and when I get damn good and ready.

He pauses recriminating me just long enough to finish his beer and order up another. After that, I cannot even think anymore, and I couldn't eat *anything* now, even if my life depended upon it.

Saturday November 22

Approaching the entrance to 20½ North Welter Street, I ran across the imp from the basement.

It was early evening.

I thought *Might she also die alone on Saturday nights, lamenting her soul's fractures?? Might she, too, have deep fissures that block her life's way...???*

She stumbled as she attempted to mount the icy cement steps, so, I asked if I might assist. As I moved closer, my senses were suddenly overrun by the heady fumes emanating from her — a Stygian mix of patchouli, reefer, sex, and booze — and for an instant, the bizarre assault literally separated me from consciousness.

She eyed me up and down, then, sneered at me contemptuously.

Look at you, you fuckin' square she slurred, **what the hell d'ya think some drag like <u>you</u>'s gonna do for <u>me</u>???**

I now keenly regretted reneging on that workout commitment I'd made, for my procrastination was plainly costing me *plenty*.

I like you I said urgently, goaded by an unearthly dementia.

THAT SMELL!!!

Let me walk you to your door???

Again, her mocking sneer, followed by a derisive shrug.

I don't care, <u>SQUARE</u>. Her words hissed through bluish paranha teeth, and a bee-stung cupid's-bow mouth.

The stiff nipples of her bra-less breasts were not masked at all by the wafer-thin jacket she wore, and its brevity brilliantly showcased high ass-cheeks that looked as tight as clenched fists. A small round scar indented the left side of her top lip, and dark spiraling curls veiled her face seductively.

This dirty waif was no beauty, but she oozed a freakish essence that I found impossibly magnetic and made me desperate to possess her. In those hooded eyes, I recognized deadly hemlock that drew me like a Siren's song, and I wanted it, for it was something I had lost. I knew its lethality, and yet, I persisted; I was powerless... I was going under.

What's your name?? I pressed, as I trailed her downstairs.

She didn't bother dignifying my question with a response, just banged on the apartment door.

A twentysomething guy with very long, very lank blond hair answered her knock, and ran insolent eyes over me as he leaned casually against the frame. He was bare-chested, and his jeans rode so low, I could see the upper margin of his pale pubic fleece. He was definitely 'looking down' on me, and although I'm nearly six feet, I'm pretty slight right now, and his towering presence dwarfed me.

Hey Hil said he, with a flip of his thumb in my direction, **what the hell is <u>this</u>?**

To my burning chagrin she replied **Just some jerk that wanted to walk me to my door.**

Together then, they shared a heartless laugh.

Come on, baby he said, smiling like a shark as he drew her inside, **papa's ready for a nice long ride...**

At that point they slammed the door; I decided that it was time to ask Floyd to brush my hair.

Sunday November 23

   You are too good for her, Amigo Floyd tells me as he brushes
and brushes my defiantly curling locks. ***You do not need her. I
am telling you, you do NOT.***

   I sit sullenly with a towel around my shoulders, my collar still
damp from when Floyd washed my mutinous hair over the kitchen sink
not much more than an hour ago.

   She is nothing like Carmen he says wistfully, as I stare into
a portable mirror at his willowy hands resting on my shoulders.

   I have still never seen his wife (who has gone to church again
tonight, to pray for his lost soul).

   That's a hundred strokes, Amigo he says, dropping his arms to
his sides with a heavy sigh after placing the brush on the counter.
He joins me at the well-worn table, and his eyes wander dejectedly
around the discolored room.

   I can no longer make her love me he mourns. ***She hates me,
Jerome. Ramon hates me, too. He is only four, and already, I make
him feel shame; I have failed.***

   I tell him he hasn't, but he insists, and to preclude him from
coming apart (like he did last week, which I could not bear again),
I point out his obvious assets. While he knows everything I say
is entirely true, I still sense that it's worlds apart from what
he intends by his statement.

   After dinner, he asks if I'll shelter him once more overnight,
and [as usual] I have nothing planned, so, I answer **Why not** — but
I make it abundantly clear (to both of us) that he will have to
sleep on the sofa, and that I will NOT be skipping work for him
again tomorrow. He nods to my terms and offers to bake us a cake,
which I accept. _My_ offer is to buy us a bottle, but then he drops
that he doesn't drink.

   Therefore, the cake (I insist) must be chocolate.

Before we wrap the night up, I agree to try washing his hair for him.

Provocatively, it ensnares my hands, my wrists, my forearms — seeming to have a life of its own — and suddenly I hate him. I hate his pristine skin and hypnotic olive eyes with their alluring shadow of lush lashes.... hate his tall, graceful body with its rippling leonine movements and that easy, regal bearing.

But then, as this malevolence kindles in my mind, I begin to consider Floyd *himSelf* — and just as suddenly, decide that perhaps I should feel for him instead.

Floyd is a mess I remind myself, now struggling to comb through skeins of wet hair, and undo all the bungling tangles I've made, *and his problems are even worse than mine.... much worse than any of mine will EVER be.*

I'm suffering like hell because some tramp has refused me, yet Floyd, exquisite as he is, cannot keep his stunning (and beloved) wife by his side, or even win the admiration of his own son.

Floyd, to whom I'm unable to resist attaching such majesty, can't bring himself to resolve his ridiculous, irrational reactions to his own exotic (and rather enviable) ethnicity.

All I've got to do is stay out of trouble, but being a "fuckin' square" leaves me wishing for death. Answering to my essence, however, threatens unfixable straits —— and this clash has begun to unmake me.

A knock on the door rescues me from my own tangled skein... one of conundrums (the solutions to which guard themselves jealously within opaque, tightly-lidded vessels).

Louise Ramillo greets me with a coy toss of bleached hair and a flash of polished teeth. I curtly ask what she wants, and though she feigns a wounded expression, I have no doubt she is *expert* at play-acting manipulative emotions. She asks if I remember her (and calls me "Jerry", which makes me detest her that much more).

If Floyd sees her, he will be all to pieces again.

I have company is my stony reply.

She tries to fondle and caress her way by me, which I impede.

What do you want? I demand.

Be my lover she coos. **I have money; I can keep you happy...
and satisfied.**

I think to myself *This cannot be real. What kind of nutty
business IS this??*

I say I don't want her money (how much could she *possibly* have anyway, living at this down in the heels dump of a building on North Welter Street... and she's got no idea that "satisfying" me, would split her like a motherfucking chicken).

When I tell her I want her to leave, she purrs that I will give in eventually....promising that she'll be back — and a nasty draft whips through the door as I shut it in her face.

Who was that? Floyd asks, upon my return to the kitchen.

Some crazy woman had the wrong place I answer truthfully.

Monday November 24

    Tonight, my seat in the kitchen finds me secretly dreading the impending Thanksgiving (which I will again have to face alone).

    I left home around three years ago, but Thanksgiving is when I most miss my gentle grandmother — so unlike the crone and her disparaging accusations.... *Old Lady Jerome!*

    I hate holidays. All of them.

    Grandmother would welcome me without reservation, but _I_ can't cope with how disappointing I have been. I was supposed to study dentistry, not go to San Francisco to "check out the scene" or to "find myself" or to "write".

    I will never detail San Francisco on these pages, even if it IS the portal to my persona, for I cannot endure its memory. It thus, remains something I will never be able to integrate — a realization that causes me great pain, for it probably means that my miserable incompleteness will indeed define my completion.

    I escaped to San Francisco in search of "my life", and instead, I *lost* it there. I must endure this banality, because I fucked up an existence better matched to me — and there is nothing I can do to remedy it. I suffer this colorless fate and call it "Death" (because I certainly cannot call it "Living").

    As my internal prison keeps my true Self invisible, *anyone* may project *any* identity upon me that they choose. Living this lie makes me feel suicidal, but if I kill myself, that means I will *unquestionably* end up dying "invisible", and if I die invisible, I risk being 'remembered' as a type of person I'd probably find even more repulsive than I currently find *myself*.....the type of person my basement neighbor is so very certain I am.

    Such a risk feels enormous to me — so important in my life, I feel ill just thinking about it... yet, I'm trapped against a fence by it.

Could I ever be like the naïve children in the filthy alley, who incorporate the dirt into their games, and thus, escape its dirtiness? Is it too late to choose that??

Perhaps the *truest* sages are the ones who know which polarity serves the authentic Self the most <u>compassionately</u>.

Walter Brandt's desperate clawing at the past he has lost, leaves it too mangled to ever again serve him; on the other hand, my own is well beyond my reach. San Francisco's jagged wound is the aching chasm I'm unable to cross — even though I know I must if I am to ever grasp my future. It's excruciating, yet its yawning depth and breadth immobilize me.

My present life, however, has become too odious to be tenable, and so, I cross-examine: *C'mon, was it <u>really</u> THAT BAD???*

Of course not, asshole I answer. *That whole business was just great, just fine....as long as you don't count grisly addictions or vile diseases; or violence, or obscenities — or devastating heartbreak.*

Or The Law with its terrifying, pernicious institutions....

As the teapot whistles, I stop paging through the dusty old photo album of my thoughts. I return it to the clandestine shelf in the back of my mind and hide it with the numbing veil.

The role of Old Lady Jerome must be played by me, as assigned.

Should've just become a dentist, *for sure*.

Tuesday November 25

It's becoming impossible to endure day after day of this miserable life of mine, wherein I am hopelessly cornered by an old identity I have no choice but to discard, and ruthlessly dominated by the distasteful thing I now consider myself.

I have begun to break apart — utterly exhausted by all the brooding I have bled out over the girl in the basement, and all the energy I've hemorrhaged despising my growing addiction to Floyd.

It should <u>not</u> then, come as the heart-stopping shock it does when in a horrifying nightmare tonight, the jailed Luther escapes and snarling, seizes me by my psyche.

Old Lady Jerome, I WILL make you face the things you refuse to, and keep this stinking key from you for <u>good</u>!! Oh yeah, I <u>will</u> replay every single scene!!!

Desperate to force the archetype from my dreams, I awaken with a start — trembling, cold, sweat-soaked, and sobbing.

I am aware that the numbing veil has indeed been ripped away, and can see the wreckage of my secret cerebral photographs now strewn far and wide across the landscape of my memory.

I have no way of escaping the sordid deeds the figure was about to recount, so, I confess them tearfully to myself, one by one, as I gather up the scattered evidence.... but I am much more humane than <u>it</u> could have afforded to be.

I avert my mind's eyes, still trying to avoid the images I have striven to suppress. I slip them back into the limbic binder inscribed with heart-rending names I remain unable to process.

Wednesday November 26

My face flushes with shock as a knock on the door rudely crashes my focused absorption. I'm startled to my senses, yet I'm frozen stupidly — rooted like a great tree, but not nearly so noble. I'd ignore the summons, but it's just too insistent...

Amigo, please let me in — I have to talk to you!

After what feels like an aeon I finally answer; I am hoping I appear composed (but suspect I'm still wearing the scarlet mask, for I can feel its heat).

Floyd's there.

(Figures....)

What's wrong? he wonders. **You are so RED.**

His face (initially enraged and indignant) has softened; he is worried about me. It allows my wits [momentary] space to regroup, and I gather them in a centering deep breath.

Nothing is wrong I lie — the familiar metallic tingling now buzzing throughout my mouth — **but what's wrong with <u>YOU</u>??**

The indignation returns; his eyes blacken with rage. It seems "that licentious Ghanaian" had the gall to proposition him AGAIN this morning, and he is *furiously* offended. He has stewed over it all day — waiting until he heard me come home, to grouse to me about it.

Confronted with this, my self-consciousness gives way to a poker-hot impatience. I am sick to death of this entirely imagined, projected burden of his. His fabulous ethnicity is both valid and intriguing — something quite special that ought to be a source of pride — and each time he's popped off one of these rankling rants, it's taken everything in my power to keep from knocking him out. Now, he has ignited my tinderbox temper once more, and once more I must smother the flashover to physical violence.

My mouth, though, spits vituperative fire.

Look here, bitch I snap, absolutely livid, *what exactly do you think it IS that makes you so fucking gorgeous??? Well, it's that black father you hate so much and that white mother of yours that was smart enough to marry his ass!! You need to get your fucking shit together and get over your goddamn self — and shut the hell up about it, too, because one day, I'm gonna really hurt you if you don't.*

He gapes at me, aghast.

If he had any idea he'd caught me jerking off, my harsh words have slapped it right out of his head. *I* have not forgotten, though, so, quickly (and much more gently) I say *Why don't you come and sit down; let me make you some tea, and we'll talk.*

As Old Lady Jerome bustles about (putting on Grandmother's tea kettle and setting out cups), I regard Floyd surreptitiously from the corners of my attention. As he watches me, his agitated, fuming bewilderment tarries, but I note that the seaweed-green is seeping back into his eyes. It means those dilated pupils are retracting as his pique slowly wanes — and *that* means that soon, he'll be able to read me.

My psychosis imagines that as Floyd's incisive gaze returns, my act will present as an actual *form* — a palpable, evident thing readily seen — just like I was wearing my soul on my sleeve. I hide my 'medicinal masturbation' (and how *much* I do it), because of the reason I have to (and as you know, my Wednesdays are HELLISH, so...)

Thank you for the tea, Jerome he says, as I sit down across from him. *I'm sorry that I have offended you.*

Despite my own shame (or maybe because of it), I decide I ought to advise.

Don't be such a fucking racist, Floyd— you KNOW how that pisses me off. And honestly, it TOTALLY detracts from your beauty. It's very ugly.

It then dawns on me I have no right whatsoever to judge him — that <u>none</u> of this is my business, for it has nothing at all to do with me. What the hell do I know about his life or any of the shit he's encountered... or for all I know, maybe *continues* to. We're united as human beings, though, in that we grapple with pain.

But pain itself is a strictly personal thing, regardless of whether it's aired openly or not — so, while I might decide that I'm 'helping' him with my "advice/opinion", I actually cannot help at all. The weighty burden of our personal suffering can only be borne privately. If anyone should know this is so, it's me.

As if in response to my thoughts, he speaks again — sad tears beginning to glisten in those veridian eyes.

I laid down with Carmen last night he tells me. *It was the first time in....months. I wanted to — I HAD to — but I could not. She spat at me and called me awful names. I have blown it, Amigo; she is leaving me. I will lose Celeste, too, and my little Ramon. What am I going to do??*

Thus, I just stare down at the plaid linoleum — awash in my own private pain... with no right at all to tell Floyd how very lucky I think he is, to have a relationship to "blow".

I don't know, Floyd I say. *I don't know.*

Thursday November 27

    It's Thanksgiving.

    In an act of self-loathing rebellion, I dined upon a pair of boiled hot dogs and some canned spinach.

    This morning, though, Floyd brought over a pie he made for me, and so (despite my holiday defiance), I still had a treat.

Happy Fucking Thanksgiving.

Friday November 28

    This Friday night, I'm petulantly watching the stupid tv and
drinking tea from the dingy white mug that's become my favorite.
I imagine my feet in a deep tub of hot water, and there's a warm
mustard plaster on my chest (like my grandmother doctored me with
one time I'd caught a deathly cold, some harsh winter years ago).
I shake the vignette, but it does seem I'm now slowly becoming her.

    I worry that the footsteps in the hall are Louise Ramillo's —
but no, it has to be Floyd; a molasses-like baritone is thrumming
a sensuous melody....and it sounds like Spanish phrasing.

    (That guy sure waxes "ethnic" despite the contempt he directs
at his forebears. It looks as though neither of us can reconcile
the thing we must "BE".)

    I stiffen a little as I hear him fitting the unfamiliar key
into the unfamiliar lock, but nevertheless, I stand by the reasons
I decided to give him that key the other night.

    Foremost, had been doing something (<u>anything</u>) that might stop
his tears, for he'd broken down after confiding the demise of his
family (and his sadness just takes me apart). My need to quell my
shame over denigrating his relationship with his personal genealogy
was up next. That is *his* business, not mine; I had no right.

    Having provided the key, however, it's since dawned on me that
he can sneak in here now and molest me....or catch me masturbating.
Although I'd be iniquitously lying if I claimed *any* alarm at the
idea of Floyd having his way with me, getting caught self-servicing
is an image that makes me full-on sick to my stomach.

    Too late, too late I ruefully acknowledge; I cannot deny how
giving away my key, amounts to a massive symbolic gesture.

    Amigo! he salutes giddily upon entering. ***It's my birthday!***

I'm frozen in my seat as I gape at an apparition of my friend.

Garish eye makeup tarnishes his lids and lovely lashes, and he has painted a small silver heart on his cheek. The stiffly teased blond wig is pretty much the tawdriest thing I have seen in a very long time — although it runs a close second to the scarlet lips, their matching ankle-length velvet dress, and choker of glittering, trashy rhinestones. A 5 o'clock shadow of facial hair warps all of it even more... his customarily meticulous shave, he has clearly forgone.

My instant reaction is knee-jerk: I am appalled.

What have you done to yourself? I say, in a voice I can barely find. **What's <u>happened</u> to you???**

I'm celebrating my birthday he declares.

Then (just like sand), a new detail abruptly stalls the gears of my aversion: Floyd is drunk.

But...you don't drink... I reflect aloud.

Oh no says he jocularly, **but tonight— Jerez!**

He staggers toward me (thank the stars, he is barefoot), and giggling, plops beside me on the sofa. In the interest of security, I take the bottle from his hand and place it on the rickety old coffee table.

Tell me Happy Birthday, Amigo he coos into my face.

Happy Birthday, Floyd I respond.

The whole scene skews surreal as I sit on the sofa with this tipsy-ass drag queen in a red velvet dress and a platinum wig (which from beneath, tendrils of long, black hair are already escaping). Floyd samples ladylike sips from my mug of tea; I take deep draughts of sherry straight from the bottle...

His head is on my shoulder now, and he sighs.

Amigo...?

Uneasily, I raise the bottle again. I cannot for the life of me, understand why I've let him rest his head there.

Amigo...?

Floyd, no. He wonders why not, and I repeat **NO**. He tells me it's his birthday, that he's twenty-eight, and that he's getting old.

No you're not I comfort, with not nearly enough comfort.

Ehh, Jerome... I thought you liked me.

When I swear I *do* like him, he wants to know why, then, I don't *want* him. Again, I upend the bottle to my mouth, beginning to feel dangerously swoozy.

As heavily as Floyd's head weighs on my shoulder, my past weighs in my heart. My present assails me, and it's not just the sweet wine besetting my stomach; I don't want to lose precious ground... I just <u>can't</u>.

It's because I'm impure, isn't it?? It's because I'm impure—

I gently assure him that it certainly is not — that HE is not, but he begins to swell with anger, accusing me of finding him unfit and filthy. He tells me how he thought I was different, how he thought I really liked him, how I've played him for a fool, for a clown.

I despise you! he shouts, leaping up in a rage, and in panic, I try to pull him back down. This is my only friend; I need him so much more than I want to, and for many more reasons than I can stand. My grasp causes him to lose his balance, and he tumbles awkwardly across my lap.

The sage eyes reach deep into my clandestine vault, tearing away the veil and scattering confidential materials everywhere. I allow him to hesitantly kiss my face, then my lips, and I'm distraught to find his trembling timidity so tender, so pleasing — for I had finally accepted that my splintered and desensitized state *is* the only safe harbor.

As I hold Floyd's long, lithe body in my arms and find myself returning his impassioned caresses, I know I'm caught in a riptide.

Saturday November 29

     I awaken today to an annoying, persistent banging that wedges
through the dim November morning and the fuggy haze in my brain.
I stir, and find Floyd's black hair tangled pleasantly across my
face like a soft, fragrant mesh; its intricacy confuses me, yet
I'm reluctant to disturb it.

     What IS *that damn* noise??? I think to myself, before finally
identifying it as a tapping on my front door.

     Sighing ruefully, I free myself from the ebony web, crawl from
the chaotic sheets, and make my way to the offending sound. I
reach for my robe as I exit the bedroom, and despite the misery of
a horrible hangover, I smile a little as I nudge the discarded wig
out of the way, with my foot.

     It's Louise Ramillo.

     Go away I say, *I'm busy.*

     Oh, you! she titters much too intimately. *You've only got on
a bathrobe — how can you be busy?? Why don't you and I DO something
this morning....George will be out all day....*

     What exactly are we supposed to be 'doing' I mock back, **when
'all you've got on, is a <u>bathrobe</u>'.**

     Indeed, I am astonished that she would come through the halls
so scantily clad — and mortified that she should be seen this way
at <u>my</u> front door.

     She teehees, calling me a charming silly as she pushes past me
into my living room. She is really starting to provoke me now—
this ugly, disgusting harpy.

Company? she inquires upon spying the red dress in its crumpled repose beside the sofa. On the coffee table, the toppled sherry bottle, lipstick-stained cup, and winking choker pose in a lewd, suggestive still life. *Is she pretty...?*

<u>VERY</u> I reply, and loading my tone with as much frosty disdain as possible, *so, would you mind <u>leaving</u>, please.*

I am thunderstruck when she tells me that yes, she WOULD mind; she would like to tell this girl about <u>US</u>.

There is no US, bitch I flare, as I shove her out of my unit. *Now fucking leave me <u>ALONE</u>!*

She flings a snarl back at me and tries very hard to slap me, but I'm able to deflect her blows. As I wrestle the door closed, she's yelling that I don't know what I'm throwing away.

Oh <u>yes</u> I do! I think to myself. *I am throwing out the <u>trash</u>!!*

I tremble with speechless rage for a moment, before I shout through that closed door *Don't you <u>EVER</u> fucking come back here!!!* but a howling tumult seems to snatch up my words and litter them.

It's evening now, and Floyd's gone back home. I don't feel like fixing dinner or sitting alone this Saturday night, so, I climb the stairs to the inverted trough of Walter Brandt's rooftop apartment, seeking accompaniment to the tavern.

Up here, it's strange and eerily silent — like the soundless "black watermelon" days I once read about. Walter Brandt knows about them, too; I spotted the book on one of his shelves amid the countless other works. I'm sure he hasn't read every book on those shelves, but I know he's read that one... I can just *tell*.

Let's go to the tavern and grab a bite I propose. He gets his peacoat and comes with me, away from 20½ North Welter Street.

At a corner table (no seats left at the bar), a waitress with ruby hair piled high, sets glasses of water before us. The poet briefly clasps her hand and addresses her as "Rose".

I think *ROSE?!? A red-haired tavern waitress named 'Rose'?? Now what sort of crazy fiction is THIS???*

She smiles dreamily at him, then walks away.

Are you writing these days? I ask, thinking it an ironically appropriate topic to induce conversation (and knowing now, that this question will not disturb him).

Not a lot he tells me with a shrug. **I'm still not ready.**

You'll <u>never</u> be ready, you old fart I sneer to myself, but to him, I just say **Oh**.

So, what's up with that family on the 2nd floor? I presently venture offhandedly (as I pause the consumption of my diner dinner to answer a vague-yet-urgent longing to in some way feel Floyd nearby). **What's their trip?**

Nice looking kids says Walter Brandt after a gulp of beer and very little deliberation. **Nice looking wife, too — or whatever she is.**

Have you ever talked with her? I pry.

I offered to be a man to her once, no more no less.

I feel perilously close to tipping my hand, but I can't seem to help pressing on.

I've heard a little about her... what does she look like?

He tells me **Eminently** fuckable — sweet, fruity-looking ass; headful of radiant dark hair. Nice fat boobs, too... big ones.

Looks real classy he says, **and <u>pricey</u>.**

He then tells me that if I'm thinking about getting next to her I might as well forget it, because she comes off **cold as a goddamn popsicle** and is **<u>W-A-Y</u> out of your league.**

He eyes me over the rims of his glasses and asks me directly, if that's why I want to know so much about her.

Oh no, no particular reason I offer. *Just wanting to know a little gossip about folks in the building.*

My wink helps to satisfy him with this, and I resume my dinner.

Rose has a decent box says Walter Brandt out of nowhere, as we walk home. *It's kinda like fucking a big ol' bath towel...you know the type — well, maybe YOU don't.... just sort of wraps around real wet and easy. She's a total square, though; insipidly straight. I am entirely too far out for her. I'm used to the fast chicks, you know — the hippie chicks.*

Oh I say, as I glance over at his grizzled ponytail and patched, faded jeans. *Oh* I say again.

I'm not at all attending the performance of Walter Brandt; I <u>cannot</u> get Floyd out of my mind. Although my addled feelings (and my diner dinner) have me a little bit queasy, I can't deny how delicious my heart finds him. His amazing face floats in my head like a drug—

—that Hillary chick.

What? I ask, spinning slowly out of my preoccupation. I have no idea how long Walter Brandt has been addressing me.

That Hillary chick — the one that lives in the basement.

A sudden bedlam obliterates Floyd's image.

*Hey, I like balling hippie chicks, but that one turned out real
nasty....AND a damn thief. I beat the crap out of that lousy bitch
— and I didn't pay her EITHER.*

<u>Pay</u> *her...??*

*Ah, she's a two-bit whore, a skag head; I've had all of 'em —
her and the whole slutty lot of 'em that hang out around here...
just a bunch of whores and boozers and hopheads. Now, don't get
me wrong, Jerome, I dig the hippies — I'm one* <u>MYSELF</u>*, mind you.
But THAT chick, though??* <u>That's</u> *the BOTTOM... that one's the* <u>WORST</u>
kind of loser.

How in the world did this come up??? When???? I'd been so
lost in my reverie I had missed it, and its lethal spike abruptly
bolts past to present.

I suggest that maybe she just can't help it, maybe she's just
kind of lost. I feel myself getting clammy, as my stomach starts
to really swim and the bedlam becomes blacker.

*Nah, she digs it. That pony-pushing pimp of hers keeps her
good and high, and plenty sexed up. I'm telling you, kiddo — that
skinny-ass bitch loves every BIT of it. You coming in for a beer?*

The LAST thing I could possibly manage this evening, is to watch
this motherfucker get soused; I am already *more* than nauseous
enough, and I'm on the edge.

He offers to get us some women.

I'm tired I say. *I'm going to bed.*

Suit yourself, but I'm damn sure having a chick to wet <u>my</u> *knob
with,* <u>this</u> *night.*

As I close my door behind me, I am so glad to get away from
Walter Brandt; I despise him.

More than anything I ever have before, I want to move away from
20½ North Welter Street.

51

When I switch on the light, I see Floyd asleep on my sofa.

    I could scream, and almost can't help doing it; I so *desperately* need privacy right now.

    I shake him roughly — awakening him, demanding he go home to his wife. He begs me to let him stay, because another man is taking Carmen and the kids out this evening, and he cannot bear being there to see it.

    Do what you did before you got <u>MY</u> door key I spit... **DO <u>THAT</u>!**

    Oh mi Amigo he pleads, **please do not make me go home!!**

    I am so tired of being confused and in pain; I am sick to death of it. Now, I am going to fight.

    Damn it, Floyd, get the hell out of here, or I'm gonna beat the living <u>shit</u> out of you—— I thunder....and the stifled tsunami of rage, lust, and grief finally breaches. As its formidable surge crashes through me, my careening emotions get swept helplessly into the hurtling, foaming rush, and my brain goes under.

    His kryptonite eyes goad me like a debauched summons; I attack furiously — ripping off his clothing, and grasping him so violently I leave bruises on that smooth, caramel skin. Driven to delirium by tortured emptiness, I've become a profane demon, and I brandish its barbed tail like a deadly dagger.

    Floyd wields the smoldering torch I at last ignite. It roars mightily to life — redeeming the caged passion that I swear to him is now his alone.

    I plunge my hands into his savage mane, and set the whole room on fire.

Sunday November 30

When I awaken this morning, I'm scarcely able to move. My body feels unendurably leaden, and my very soul aches from last night's impiety. The dagger is gone.

A dim predawn depicts the bedroom in flat charcoals — imparting a faded color to Floyd's slumbering form. The mesh of black hair tangled across my face, is no longer pleasing; it feels as thorny as November's gnarled fingers.

The chasm leers, and I see all the way down into its sickening maw.

At the bottom (beside the charred remains of my prison), Floyd's gallant torch lies extinguished.... but my duplicitous vows have absconded. That oath to him and the deeper one to myself (the one to exile my unlivable "lifelessness") stole away as I slept.

It appears I have managed to betray us both, and there is not a blessed thing I can do about it.

There is no point in yearning to exist beyond Saturday night sock-sewing, or tea in the yellowed kitchen... beyond watching the children with their trashcan fortresses and guns of sticks... beyond the inane tv. From its distant origin in hell, November's bleak light adds moody shadows to the chiaroscuro that illustrates my world — so twisted and so static; there is just no point.

I hate everything I think.

Floyd stirs; he strokes me.

Buenos dias, Amigo.

His gooey voice becomes brittle as it strikes the unyielding starkness of my reality and then shatters into the icy shards that cut me. I rise slowly from the bed and notice it's snowing outside, before hobbling stiffly into the kitchen to fix tea and breakfast. There will be no torrid love scenes this morning.

As I place a cup before him, Floyd asks what is wrong — if he has done something to upset me — and I tell him **No** as I set our plates on the table.

He presses me more directly.

It's that girl in the basement, isn't it.... You are in love with her.

Floyd, I'm not I respond; there is no sign of tingling vibration. **Please eat.**

He does not eat but gets up slowly, and I have never seen him look so despondent.

You don't want me anymore, do you he implores, and I must tell him **Floyd, I just can't.**

You have not been fair to me he says, without the familiar pet name, Amigo, which I have come to treasure. He calls me instead, a wicked boy. He wants to know why I've toyed with him, why I pretended to fall for him... why I promised myself to him, when I had never meant it. He tells me I should have never made love to him in the first place... and he is right.

As we leave the kitchen, I offer a shirt to replace the one I so brutally rent last night, but he refuses it — and I ask him (although I have no right to) **What will you do now?**

He has no idea how desperately my ruined heart calls out to him, how ineptly it strives to not be swept away in the awful gulf widening so inexorably between us, and the riptide that now carries me away from him; he has no idea why I have to let him go...or why I'm unable to explain it.

Carmen is leaving me he says wearily; *she's taking the children. There is a man— a businessman— older— that wants me to come to him— and now... I guess I will have to do it. He is not appealing, and I actually cannot stand him...*

He turns his head, but not before I see the tears in his seafoam eyes. I want to take him in my arms and love him, to keep him safe right here with me in my secluded little apartment.... away from Carmen and the hideous old businessman.... away from everything.

Instead, I stand stoic — watching him walk down the hall — and I stay there until I hear his door close. It shuts out the chance I will ever get to see him again, and locks in the fact that he will become yet another of my aching memories.

November's wind whistles drearily as I return to the kitchen and fall apart privately.

Monday December 1

    November at last folds away her mantle of bitterness, and
December ascends the throne; the vicious winds bow as she arrives,
clad in frosty, silent crystals.

    The gray alley behind 20½ North Welter Street has turned white,
and the trashcans are now snugly blanketed in her glittering cloak.

    The sticks have all been covered.

    Winter is indeed upon us, as another chapter ends.

PART II

THE WEIGHT

FORGE

this furnace of pain

bestows illumination

as it tempers me

                        -Jerome 1972

Although Springtime has begun to rule the days, on many nights Winter yet walks. Her cold footsteps cast rime across the grass, but at dawn she must yield — and her tears become trembling dew as she grieves that unwilling departure.

Nonetheless, impatient Spring continues to advance.

She raises the heaven and dots the awakening earth with buds and sprigs and green clusters. All things seem to broaden or bloom when Springtime is running the show.

Her verdant breath is everywhere; it permeates me, and I cannot help but dare resume my journey.

Thus, another chapter...

Tuesday April 20

Well, today I spotted Floyd.

I'd been walking with Jenny in Peril's Park (a charming oasis smack in the midst of the city's bustling heart) because at 4:30 when we finished up work this afternoon, it was just so wonderfully warm outside, I'd suggested we stroll over there to sit and unwind, and later, maybe even grab a nosh at the tavern.

The 'park' is really a pair of pastoral square lawns, each one bounded by the pavements of a midtown block but secluded from these by low shrubberies. They nestle on either side of a one-way street headed north — a busy artery that's almost always congested (partly because its two skimpy lanes are so cartoonishly narrow, and partly because a stoplight [mercifully] jams up the traffic... otherwise the poor pedestrians would *never* get across it).

Both bucolic siblings are quaintly appointed with birdbaths and statues, and are framed by trees, and by rough old wooden benches (which are painted the dark color of a cucumber's skin and have a remarkably similar texture).

By day, the park's a popular alfresco haven — especially for workers from the many adjacent office buildings, who picnic their take-out lunches and try to snatch a few rays. After dark, however, it crawls with the dopers, dealers, and hustlers that compete for the benches with homeless people who are congregating to crash (as the public library is closed in the evenings).

It's this seedy assemblage that first led me to dub the place "Peril's Park".... and if you're smart, you *will* stay out of there once the sun has gone to bed.

Jenny is my new coworker; she joined our small staff at the magazine collection center just over a month ago. We hit it off in the cheerless little lunchroom one day, upon discovering that another soul working there had actually read a book, and was eager to discuss something besides the weather (or whatever tv show happens to be popular at the moment).

Since then, we've been hanging out not only at lunch, but after most shifts as well — so (understandably), she imagines herself my girlfriend..... and I allow her this. I liken Jenny's arrival to the great St. Bernards of legend: showing up heroically bearing the mythical 'keg of brandy' thought to warm away the lethal cold while a downed traveler waited for rescue.

When we met, it was the first time I'd responded to *anything* after losing Floyd last November. I'd put my heart in deep-freeze to kill that agony, but I was numbing myself to death; I owe Jenny big-time for the 'warming help' of her friendship, and I know it.

...Speaking of 'help'...

Back in December, my 'therapist' had zealously applauded my resolve to relinquish Floyd.

(My probation compels the edgy sessions I must endure with this person whose purpose is twofold: dismantle my savagely righteous temper and delete my rampaging sexuality. Both of these, she maintains, trace back to the same source — my ruptured home and its [inevitable] abandonment issues.

My satyriasis, says she, is simply another of my "acts of angry defiance"; it is calculated and deliberate — a symptom of the resentment she is so certain I harbor against my natural parents for their "enraging absence". It matters not one bit to her that my beloved grandmother is all the parent I have ever needed; the rife resentment I do harbor is directed at this therapist *herself* for daring to denigrate that precious bond.)

Ms. Therapist damn-near erased me; she had me so knotted up and disordered, I didn't even know who I was anymore. She convinced me that my "aberrant" bisexuality was a fiction, and my same-sex "insistence" was merely a predictable extension of my rebellious nature — a condition from which I (presumably) could recover, and it was *her* job to make sure that I did.

The catastrophies I suffered in San Francisco, in her opinion, were all tied to my [tragic] gravitation toward *men*. If I'd just not do *that*, everything would magically change for me; I would meet a nice girl and not lose her if/when I got her pregnant....because we could get married, and everything would go happily ever after.

Heeding her is how I lost Floyd; I let her confuse me... and I destroyed us.

In revenge, I strive to appall and offend her as best I can, because "The System" might make me talk to her, but it damn sure cannot make me be sweet. There is no way in fuck I am *ever* letting that bitch back in my brain, just so she can wreck it again.

Ms. T was *thrilled* when I had met Jenny. Here at last was that 'regular' girl for me to take up with — someone "nice", not slutty or 'fast'....or hot-blooded, like myself. Most importantly, Jenny was *female,* which of course (to Ms. T), was the most winning asset of all.

Jenny *is* a nice girl, and I like her, but my feral intensity will only torch her; there's just no way she's built to weather the blistering firestorm I will take her through.

Today, as we waited at the stoplight between the park's east and west sisters, I'd been vacantly observing the length of storefronts that line the busy artery. On the right, just before the next cross street, is a pharmacy, and I saw Floyd exit its door and fold up into the passenger side of a pepper-red sports car, its drop-top down. I couldn't see much of the driver (who was obscured from my view by the roll-bar).

My heart launched into my throat and wedged there; I literally could not breathe. Jenny towed me (I guess?) to a bench and sat me down. I don't even remember getting to it.

She kept clasping my hands as I fought against abject despair that was crammed with tears — confidential tears I was determined Jenny mustn't by <u>ANY</u> means, ever get to see. She knows nothing of my past (or present, for *that* matter), and I certainly didn't want her to know I am vulnerable. A mere *glimpse* of Floyd had just full-on disabled me, which was embarrassing and sickening all at once; I *had* to have some time alone to process the whole business privately.

I'd frightened Jenny so badly, though, _she_ had determined that by <u>NO</u> means whatsoever, should I be left by myself.

I told her I sometimes get weird panic attacks, yet the triggers remain unknown (because they occur so randomly, you see). I said I was in therapy for help with this, and that I'd actually expected to have it resolved _way_ before she'd ever have the misfortune of seeing one.

I apologized for alarming her — swearing everything was okay and that I'd be perfectly fine on my own. It had been a long day, I explained, since I woke up earlier than usual this morning; I was probably just a lot more bushed than I'd realized.

All I needed, I then calmly guaranteed her, was to hit the hay — and she bought it.

I waited at the stop with her, for the bus that would carry her back uptown to where she lived with her parents. She gave me a little kiss goodbye and clasped my hands again before boarding. I made sure to wait until I saw her seated and waving from her window, then, I left to go home.

...My mouth is _still_ fucking buzzing...

Wednesday April 21

   Therapy Day.

   Today, I spent our entire half-hour lunch break laughing and
joking with Jenny — bent upon allaying any lingering concerns she
might be having about my 'episode'. I had to be careful, for while
she's only nineteen (and a particularly *young* nineteen at *that*,
having been, it's clear, sheltered to an extreme by her parents),
Jenny's no dummy. If I'd seemed just a little *too* glib, she might
have scrutinized me more closely than I thought wise to risk.

   Predominating the *back* of my mind all day, has been what I plan
to say to Ms. T at my weekly appointment (every damn Wednesday
right after work). I'd love to tell her the truth (that'd *REALLY*
get her going), but if I tell her the truth, she will feel a need
to 'treat' me and I just could not bear it. I don't need anybody
trying to analyze this thing for me....*especially* <u>HER</u>.

   I decide to go with a half-truth: that I had an impromptu date
with Jenny yesterday afternoon, and it got cut short when I suddenly
felt sick. Ms. T knows my insides act up, so, this will fly with
her. Then, I will tell her how well Jenny and I got along today —
how we laughed and joked all through lunch. I can easilly fill a
fifty-minute session with more than enough credible candied fluff
to keep her off my ass until next Wednesday; she will be happy,
and I will be free of her meddling.... it's a win/win.

   Ms. T *WAS* very happy with my story. She told me how proud she
was of me—how proud she was that I was becoming so friendly and
open, and eschewing my "deeply private brooding".

   I think what she was *really* proud of, was that she imagined the
'good' results she saw in me were a direct result of her own
intervention. In other words, it was really *herself* of which she
was so proud. She never once suspected that those good results
were nothing more than a carefully crafted veneer.

It was perfectly fine with me that she go on thinking the way
she did.

The fact is, I deliberately contrived to help keep it exactly
that way — because last night (during a protracted period of
deeply private brooding), I'd realized that I was prepared to move
heaven and earth to hold Floyd in my arms again — and that it would
be much easier for me to get there, if Ms. T's thought-processes
did not follow me.

After lying sleepless in their bed for the last few hours, Floyd finally sat up and stared at the slumbering mound next to him.

Chadwick Winston dozed peacefully, emitting contented little snores with each of his light, even breaths. The sounds were minute, but tonight they raked Floyd's restive nerves like nails scraping down a chalkboard.

Eh, certainly he is happy he growled to himself, then halted his thoughts abruptly, lest he relive the moments that had led the man to such serenity.

He slipped quietly from the bed and padded down the long hallway to the enormous living room. Tonight, he actually wished he was a drinker — wished he could just numb away this distressing unrest, and float off to la-la-land, like Chad. For some reason, his conditioned capacity to erase the wafting, shadowy impressions of Jerome from his thoughts, was failing.

Agreeing to live here had not been an easy choice. Even as Carmen deserted him (and Jerome's passion so mysteriously evaporated), Floyd truly expected to somehow find a way to survive on his own without *any* of them. Although he'd told Jerome he planned to move in with the businessman, he'd still secretly held out hope he would find the wherewithal not to….but he didn't.

For what now seemed an eternity (had it really only been a few months??) he had endured this relationship in which he could not love. Yes, it had its perks (this impressive penthouse, for example, and generous gifts), but not only did his heart not belong to Chad, it lingered with Amigo. The quick-tempered youngster (with those soulful gray eyes, that wide mouth, that stoked-furnace libido) held it fast.

Floyd opened the grand sliding doors, stepped out onto the balcony overlooking the glimmering lights of the city, and selected a chaise. He reclined there awhile, breathing deeply the night's cool darkness — allowing a nebulous essence moving within its powerful stillness, to suffuse his unsettled mind.

It was there that Chadwick found him the next day... fast asleep and naked — his long body gilded by the early morning sunlight.

Sunday April 25

     Today is Easter.

     This morning, the defiantly warm weather we've been enjoying
lately, succumbed to a bitter-cold fog surge. I'm glad to use it
as a pretext to cocoon indoors and 'recluse' myself in privacy.

     Jenny had begged me last Friday, to spend all this Easter Sunday
with her relatives.

     The plan was: I should attend church with Jenny and her parents,
and then, we would all schlep over to her married sister's house
for Easter brunch with *that* family.

     It's <u>entirely</u> my fault that she'd think I might be cool with
such a thing, since I have hidden every vital detail about myself
from her. Why *wouldn't* she think I'd be up for that? I allow her
to believe our "thing" is a lot more than I know it will ever be,
and that I'm just some nice boy raised-up right by his sweet ol'
grandma. I even brush my hair sometimes now (although I continue
spurning Ms. T's efforts to convince me to cut it off).

     I opted to tell the truth about this one; I confessed I honestly
wasn't ready to take a step like that. A day such as she proposed
held a great deal of symbolic weight for me, I explained sincerely,
and it was just too early in our relationship for that kind of
move. I assured her there'd be other, less dramatic opportunities
for me to meet her folks.

     She'd been *most* disappointed — but her phenomenal intelligence
[nevertheless] won the day.

     This cat-and-mouse game I'm playing is abhorrently sinful, but
I've let her think she's my girlfriend, and thus, she (rightly)
expects our relationship will continue to "deepen"....something my
heart, though, now knows won't (can't) go down the way she imagines.

     I really *don't* know what I'm going to do about Jenny.

I *like* her. I dig engaging with her intellect, I dig her
laughter, and I dig her reliable proximity. I dig the adorable
prettiness of her earnest little face, and while her body's not
the whiplash type that usually sends me, it's extremely voluptuous,
and I would *LOVE* a chance at it.... but that's <u>another</u> problem:
there is no way in the world I have *any* business fucking this girl.
The *last* thing I need to do, is end up getting down with Jenny.

HER behavior is so amorous, though, I know she's thinking hard
about it. It's springtime, after all, and the warming weather's
got everyone frisky. She likes to sit close beside me in the park
and stroke all up and down my thighs with her warm, cushiony hand,
then, tease with shy kisses and sexy whispers — like something
out of a giddily frothy "rom-com" feature film. She has no clue
the gravely concentrated biology she is dealing with, in me.

Also, she's admitted that she is a virgin, and if *that's* not a
blaring alarm against wading in any deeper, I've <u>no</u> idea what is.
I CANNOT have her old man coming after me with a shotgun.

If I resist her, she will pursue me, and if I reject her, she
will be hurt. If I hang around, I am going to fuck her — for I
will have to — and if I fuck her, I will get her pregnant....and
THAT, I must by ALL means, avoid. (What went down with Claudia...
well, as you know, a fractured element within me might be always
too broken to bear reconciling that chapter.)

A rubber, however, will deaden the electric of coital communing
(that charged, white-hot voltage of flesh meeting flesh) and
nothing else comes <u>anywhere</u> close to it. I could wear the thing
(although I've busted through more than a few in my day) and at
least *try* to keep Jenny from getting knocked up...but then, her
"first time" will lack that singular intimacy, AND I'll have stolen
her chance to experience it sparkling brand-new and thrilling—
with someone who genuinely loves her, and thus, deserves the honor
of taking her there.

It's crossed my mind, though, that maybe I'm just spouting these
'moral' excuses, to justify releasing her (and any responsibility
I might have <u>to</u> her), because such an emotional obligation will
definitely weigh me down.

I want to be free to go after Floyd without dragging around a ton of guilty baggage.

It seems that no matter how hard I try not to, I always end up hurting someone, and I'm loath to have to carry that kind of blame again — but it's impossible to envision how this welter resolves successfully, when we're working together and seeing each other every single day.

Ms. T will flip her damn wig if I break up with Jenny, and I can't escape by job-hopping, because that will freak out my parole officer. Their [over] reactions can only mean huge setbacks for me, so, obviously, I have no other choice right now than continue playing along with everyone.... and I must hold my own cards exceptionally close, as I forge steadfastly ahead.

I can feel myself clearing the psychic space around me — which usually means I'm coming in hot.

I'm still formulating a plan for finding Floyd *physically*, but telepathically, I've already filled every airspace.

He *must* have at least a vague sense by now, that I am calling to him.

Monday April 26

Jenny was kind of aloof this morning, and I suspected it was because yesterday she'd gotten the 3rd degree. I should've been expecting this attitude (since I hadn't the decency to attend that big shindig they'd cooked up for my 'introduction').

The weather was still pretty nasty today, which meant that at lunchtime, we couldn't just go out and walk around as a distraction from each other; it meant we were stuck face to face indoors, in that godforsaken breakroom. When I asked her directly **What gives with the cold shoulder??** she crossly confirmed my suspicions.

All damn day, she'd had to field queries about my absence and why I chose not to come. My rebuff had thoroughly embarrassed her (since she'd talked me up so much and gotten them all super-hyped to finally get to meet me).

I wanted to tell her *You see,* THIS *is why we are wiser to keep these things* <u>private</u>*...* but I realized *that* particular angle would likely only escalate the matter. Instead, I gently suggested that maybe it might work better if she just held back even a *smidge* more from them. What's between US is between <u>US</u> — and leaking it out everywhere, only serves to dilute its power.

My proposal was that she feed them mere morsels — it would keep them intrigued and let their anticipation build up (**like sexual tension** I'd added, to help sell it). That way, the energy could gather where it belonged: in *our* connection with each other. She dug this, and it seemed to satisfy and relax her.

I truly wasn't lying; any shot we even *might* have (a *long* shot, indeed) would have to ripen fully beyond the reach of her folks. She would need to love me enough to stand against them — for they were going to know instantly, the minute they saw me, that I was NOT what they wanted for their daughter.

Then, she said there was going to be a war protest this weekend in Peril's Park, and that she was going, and that she hoped I would at least join her for *that* — especially since I lived so close by.

My blood went HYPOTHERMIC.

Of course, I'd heard about the protest; I had prudently planned to hide out at home. There's no *way* I could let myself get caught *anywhere* near a hotspot like that... they'd build a jail for me and put my name right on the front of it.

She'd altogether cornered me; I was going to have to come clean, and my mind raced with calculations. At issue was whether or not I should go with telling her *everything*.

A devious part of me seized upon this. If I told her everything — every sordid bit of who I was — maybe she'd be so repulsed, she'd rescind her friendship and just walk away. It would eliminate all my worries, and leave me free to go find Floyd and beg him to take me back. Would even Ms. T be able to fault me for losing Jenny because I'd merely been truthful*???* (I'll tell you <u>one</u> thing... she had better not try it.)

The plan was brilliantly simple, but would it work? What if Jenny decided she wanted to "stand by me" — her afflicted, flawed boyfriend*??*

I thought, then, that maybe I *should* talk to Ms. T about it before I gave Jenny an answer. I would let Ms. T tell me what to do, since she's supposed to be so fucking smart——but I quickly realized she'd think it'd be great if Jenny wanted to stand by me, and that she'd say it would strengthen our bond.

Nope, Ms. T was not hearing about this gnarly little crunch.... except the part that I managed to stay away from that damn protest.

Jenny I said, **I can't go to the protest. I'm on probation.**

I don't know which gaped wider, her eyes or her mouth.

I told her I didn't want to talk about it at work, but that we could hit the tavern after, and I would explain. (Luckily, it was too cold today for the park, and so, I would not have to brave her rubbing on my thighs while I struggled to suppress yet another merciless boner.)

I'd have loved to put off this particular chat, but I knew it was better to just go ahead and get it over with, to just let the chips fall. I at least took comfort in the fact that there was little chance we'd run across Floyd at the tavern — especially if he was rolling as high as that sportscar implied.

I wondered how many of those red roadsters could be 'living' around the area...

The waxy bag Floyd was holding when he came out of the pharmacy, looked like the kind they use for prescriptions. I have no way of guessing the prescribee — but if that is their drug store, I think it's quite safe to assume they reside (or at least, *work*) locally... which helps me refine my plans.

Over dinner, I explained to Jenny about the principled ethics my grandmother had instilled in me, and how I had so unwisely laced my volatile temper up in them. I told her that San Francisco had been a field of fertility for such subversive seeds as mine, and that I had gone out there intending to be a warrior and a scribe — but I kept getting into trouble, and amassed too many arrests.

What I withheld from her is that I'd ended up a wasted junkie, a rank, unhealthy skag rat..... and one of the most depraved hookers to ever prowl the dark alleyways; that also, I am crazy.

I watched her reactions carefully, and was deeply dismayed when her clear blue eyes misted over — with fascination, with empathy... with LOVE.

Jenny I said, **please don't tell your parents about any of this. PLEASE, PLEASE say that you won't.**

She promised she would not breathe a single word, and I knew she meant it.

She informed me that she would tell her parents she was going to the park for the protest, but that she would come spend the day at my place instead.

Tuesday April 27

    Springtime's advance has definitely paused, and the early buds
quiver in suspense. The cold wave persists, and its dreary interval
lends the handy screen that helps to shield my stratagems.

    I know Jenny imagines I'm a fairly "standard-issue" sort of guy
(in other words, hopelessly inept around the house), and *that*, of
course, works to my advantage as I endeavor to hold her at bay
until this [fateful] weekend.

    I have told her I want to use all my after-work time this week
to get my place spick-and-span for her visit Saturday.... that this
colder weather is perfect for such an activity, and isn't, after
all, very conducive to strolling in the park or exploring oddball
little shops. Far superior conditions for *these* will surely return
before long.

    My housekeeping habits, though, are *not* like those of a typical
bachelor my age, and as far as cleanliness and order go, my place
is already in pretty good shape. My grandmother was fastidious,
and she taught me well — often praising me for being so willing
(and able) to meet her high, exacting standards of how a home ought
to be kept.

    How I *plan* to use the time, is to comb the whole downtown area
block by block — checking everywhere I can imagine the red sportscar
might be parked.   I carefully noted the day I saw it at the
pharmacy, too, because I have every intention of haunting the place
the same time next month, when a refill of that prescription could
very well be due.   (That is, if I've not already *found* Floyd by
then....because I certainly intend to <u>have</u>.)

    It's supposed to be misting and raw this evening — a good time
to stay off the streets (or at least, not be out cruising around
in your drop-top). If it's parked anywhere along my "Day 1" route,
I will find it.

I'm hoping it won't be *too* hard, then, to figure out which building its owner might occupy. I'll just try to decide what looks posh enough, or simply 'feels' to me like the best match.

My tense excitement is almost palpable, and I let Jenny think it's all about Saturday. She is so eager for our rendezvous, and that would be dear, if *I* was not so stressed out and apprehensive.

I'm walking a razor's edge right now as I struggle to balance worry about how I'll handle having her so close to me (and my <u>bed</u>) all day long, and my impatience to get going on my search.

She's tried to hang out this entire week, but I've stayed her with a 'koan' I learned from an old friend back in San Francisco: **"The longer you wait, the hotter it gets"**

There's not nearly enough room on this razor's edge for the two of us, but she is sure putting in a potent effort to join me there.

Wednesday April 28

Therapy Day.

The minute I take my seat across from Ms. T, she can tell something's up. She sits looking at me but says nothing... a challenge to spill my guts (to relieve the ballooning pressure that accrues within the belly of our silence). I decide I'll go ahead and blink first; I'm not fucking scared of her, and I know exactly what she's doing.

I know also, that she is no match for my cunning.

Jenny's coming on Saturday to spend the day with me at my place I say. *She wanted me to join her at the war protest this weekend, so, I had to tell her why I couldn't do it. And then, when I said I had planned to stay safely at home, she invited herself over.*

Amused and smugly vindictive, I watch as Ms. T's eyebrows shoot all the way up to her hairline. Momentarily, she's lost for words, and even this *tiny* victory gives me creamy pleasure. She recovers swiftly, though, as might be expected, and of course, begins to probe.

Well, Jerome, what do you THINK about that?

I tell her I'm glad I have the common sense to stay as far away as possible from this protest. I explain how very hard I was trying to act responsibly, and that I'd never imagined Jenny would (inadvertently) place me in such a precarious position..... but that I was working very consciously not to blame her (or hold her in any contempt) for having done so.

She asks me why I had not simply told Jenny I was unavailable.

Well, touché, Ms. T.

This angle of attack, I'd not anticipated, but I quickly parry by laying out the whole Easter fiasco (offering Ms. T the same explanation I had given Jenny — that the move was too symbolic and important for this early stage of our relationship).

Letting Jenny come over this Saturday, I confess, allows me to assuage my guilt. While *I'M* not yet ready to take that big step, I *do* get how invested <u>SHE</u> had been in it, and I just cannot square disappointing her a second time.

Ms. T expresses her disappointment that I had decided against accepting the invitation Jenny's family had extended me [to share their glorious holiday with them]. She thinks it would have been "a very good exercise" for me to have gone along, but she has no choice but to allow me the space of this very personal discomfort I hold about an undertaking of such undeniable magnitude.

She then (of course) says **Let's explore this further, Jerome** and once again I find the truth my most effective weapon.

I convey that keeping Jenny from getting hurt is pretty much my top priority, and thus, how important it is to me that I am not out ahead of myself before I know exactly how I feel and what commitment level I can back up. Such an approach, I assert, evinces control and maturity of which I can (and deserve to) be proud.

Naturally, she is powerless to refute any of this, and I win the round.

Last night's clammy search served only to chill me to the bone (its futility, further deepening the icy dampness). I've been achy all day (and a little depressed, too), but none of that stops me from hitting the streets again the moment I emerge from therapy, and going right back to my quest.

This dismally drizzling cold evening, though, the quadrant I've just trekked has turned out to be yet another dud. Soaked through one *more* time (and miserable), I turn the corner to head for home and that is when I see it.

The electrified red is unmistakable; that car stands alone from every single other vehicle, even though they're lining each curb from end to end on both sides of the block. The thing looks like it must be made of light itself.

To focus on *anything* is suddenly impossible, for all my senses have become muffled by the deafening thunder of my heart.

I am literally spinning in circles as the scene morphs into a freakish wide-angled whirl of one ritzy high-rise after another — and there are so many cars parked out here, it's *beyond* far-fetched to imagine *any* of them might be in front of their own residence.

Behind which of these doors is Floyd*?!?*

It takes everything within me to repel a steamrolling urge to just stand in the street and start yelling his name at the top of my lungs. I shove my fingers in my mouth and bite down, because that's the *only* way I manage to keep it closed.

Okay... okay... Okay, bud, so, you found it. Now, slow down.... s-l-o-w...d-o-w-n.... Let's try to get smart about this...

I stroll the long block as casually as I'm capable, and observe the license tag number — waiting until I get to the corner before (*just* as casually) entering it into the little notepad I like to carry. I also record the street name and the cross streets.

Then, I open my heart's intuition and scan each building again — making sure to quiet my fiery nerve endings this time, so that I can 'hear' more effectively.

The address 2016 has sent for me.

Floyd was Chad's envied trophy — admired by the wealthy man's circle for his exotic mystique and dignified air, and a rare ability to remain so elegantly poised, yet chatter so entertainingly about things that mattered not a bit. The elite group especially favored luxe dinner socials, and for these in particular, Floyd's handsome gentility had become very much in demand among Chad's many well-heeled friends.

He sat opposite Chad and one of them now, as the trio dined together in Chadwick's penthouse this chilly Wednesday night. Floyd laughed lightheartedly at their jokes and looked appropriately alluring, as the two men endeavored to train him to enjoy just a bit of bubbly (Chad's intoxicant of choice). The thought was that while he did not consume spirits, perhaps Floyd might nonetheless find the ticklish spume at least pleasurable—if not outright fun—were he to give it a fair chance.

Subliminally (although Floyd had astutely assessed this), Chad was stalked by a feeling of inferiority, and thus, its adjunct inability to trust. Not only was Floyd's beauty superlative, his *sobriety* also gave him an undeniable edge over Chad— for he always retained the fullness of his powers, while Chadwick's requisite control was attenuated by the alcohol he so enjoyed imbibing. That his command of any situation was jeopardized, ate at Chadwick, for it projected his covert vulnerability back onto himself.

This evening, Floyd *did* use the men's tipsiness to his advantage. He was easily able to perform more than glibly enough for their bleary perceptions, while devoting nearly all of his energy to the formless disquiet that was increasingly dominating him… that had preyed upon him unremittingly, for over a week now.

Jerome seemed forever with him these days — dogging every stride, hidden in every crowd, caressing him in every shower. Floyd paced the floor and prowled the balcony like the caged animal he felt… forcing himself to not let those footsteps carry him back to North Welter Street.

Chadwick had begun to notice this distracted attention and had started watching him warily. As gorgeous as Floyd was, it was not inconceivable that he might have many solicitations to cheat —— although the businessman realized that Floyd was smart enough to know on which side his bread was buttered, and delighted in luxury enough to keep it that way. Still, Chad surreptitiously scrutinized all his associates, just in case he might catch one of them exhibiting suspicious behavior…like trying to tempt away his prize.

What's the matter, my pet? he inquired of Floyd once their dinner guest had gone. Having achieved sufficient intoxication, he now felt bold enough to venture beyond the comfortable bounds of his familiar power-zone.

Floyd responded with his most demure, disarming smile, saying ***Why would you think there is something wrong, My Friend? I'm sorry I did not drink with you tonight…… I just don't like the taste – you know that.***

His nickname for Chad was always "My Friend". He had assigned it early on in their relationship and was scrupulously careful not to ever use it with anyone else — even though it would have seemed perfectly natural.

It would have also seemed perfectly natural for Spanish-fluent Floyd to refer to Chad (or any of his crowd) as "amigo", and in fact, Chad even tried it once on *Floyd*. The pet name, however, belonged only to Jerome — and Floyd had hidden it away in his heart, where it was held in a secret trust. His reaction when Chad had used it was so vicious, Chad's 'Pavlovian reflex' had been to instantly eliminate the word from his entire lexicon. He assumed that the venomous response must have had something to do with the younger man's ethnicity.... a thing Floyd flatly declined to discuss with him.

As he considered Floyd's last statement, Chadwick had a keen sense he'd just been deflected —— yet he could find no contestable holes in the simple explanation. He decided, then, upon a different angle from which to pursue the issue.

You've seemed troubled lately, love; I'm starting to worry about you.

Indeed, his worry had begun when he'd found Floyd asleep out on the balcony that warm Friday morning… just days before Easter.

Chad *was* conscious of his lover's profound earthy streak — one that required fresh air and lots of space to move around within. It wasn't entirely out of character Floyd might opt to sleep outside, but that eerie image of him out there naked remained as unsettling (and alarming) now, as when Chad had first encountered it.

He wasn't concerned that Floyd might have felt feverish, or even worried about what neighbors might think (since the balcony was quite private). It had to do with a spookish notion that Floyd was exposing himself to something.... something in the air.... something beyond the here-and-now place everyone else occupied.

The portly industrialist was not the least bit abstract, and thus, had no way of understanding (much less, accommodating) this incredibly unnerving feeling.

The tall, winsome man approached Chadwick and draped his supple arms intimately around his neck. Chad encircled Floyd's waist with his own much more corpulent appendages, fingering the silky black hair as it spilled over his hands.

Don't worry about me, My Friend. It's only a touch of spring fever... everyone has got it; we are all just wishing the season will come and stay.

Floyd backed his reassuring words with a credible kiss, and drew his partner even closer— wrapping him up in caramel magic, and disabling any further questions or resistance, with a sultry, jade-eyed hypnosis.

Friday April 30

    I felt a little bit better this morning.

    Yesterday, my exposure to the elements over the past few nights
really caught up with me. The mountainous cold I'd come down with,
I could no longer deny; its deep chills and runny sniffles had me
too ill to even write in my journal.

    I'd fought through my symptoms, though, for I dared not call in
sick to work, and I certainly did not want Jenny to think I was
looking for an excuse to avoid her. Much better, I had decided,
to let her see how bad I was really feeling and make sure my boss
knew just how contagious I might be to the rest of [his] staff.

    Everyone I ran into had playfully (but not really so playfully)
made the sign of the cross with their fingers and given me a wide
berth... all except Jenny, of course. I seriously believe she'd
have insisted upon dying along with me if things had come to that—
and so, not only did I feel like shit, I also felt like a cad.

    Yet, I felt 'lighter' — and there's no doubt that finding the
elusive sportscar the other night (and having *some* idea where Floyd
might be) uplifted me. Once Saturday was finally finished, I
intended to climb right back into the saddle and head out on my
next course of action... which I planned to settle upon, on Sunday.

    By quitting time, the fine weather was back with a flourish.

    High above the urban landscape, the sun dazzled in a sky of
infinite blue with floating islands of cotton ball clouds. The
lively air thrilled with the green zest of spring foliage, and that
dark, transportive fragrance of damp earth.

    Jenny insisted we visit the park for a little while after work,
suggesting that the warm sun might be good for my cold and help
raise my flagging spirits. She also wanted to have a look at any
preparations being made for the protest tomorrow, as she intended

to gather specifics that would help deceive her parents. It all
sounded harmless enough, and I figured that maybe a bit of sunshine
and some fresh air might actually do me a world of good.

I was supine on one of the benches (my head in Jenny's lap, my
eyes contently closed) as she hovered over me, toying with my mad
hair — when seemingly from nowhere, a reverberant timpani voice
suddenly rumbled **Lute???...Is that <u>you</u>, Lute????**

My eyes flew open, and I sat up with a jolt.

Back in San Francisco, I'd adopted the name "Luther Pen" (which
paired my cherished childhood archetype with my writing ambition).
My group of friends affectionately referred to me as "The Bard",
but when I met David, he decided *that* took too long to say, and
thought it would be clever to compress the whole concept. He began
calling me "Lute" — contracting Luther, and assigning the bard's
classic instrument. Everyone loved it, and the nickname stuck.

I'd fallen so hard for him, back then.

Towering and criminally handsome, with an easy, engaging laugh
and a charged presence as "larger-than-life" as his staggering
kinetic intelligence, David was a true freak, to boot.

He had an avid taste for what he called "cracker tail", and
this impossibly magnetic black man was not particular about which
gender that tail might chance to be attached. He was more than
unvarnished about getting off on "white folk" bowing down to his
indisputable prowess.... and I had been <u>more</u> than happy to comply.
He'd often tell me that I was his favorite, because I was game for
pretty much any of his manifold licentious whims.

I was *irretrievably* stuck on him, and I was not just smitten
with his sizzling smarts — David <u>SENT</u> me. His decadent appetites,
unique stamina, and incredible physical assets, slaked the ravening
pathologic lust that had me always circling the rim of desperation.

He muted my aching loneliness; I could not get enough of him....
and my jealousy was <u>torrid</u>.

After a while, he'd had it with my terrifying temper (which
raged out of control whenever he'd choose anyone that wasn't me).
He decided I'd be much easier to handle if I was sedated, and thus,
began to subdue my violence with a soporific regimen of smack.

It meant he had kept me, and that was the only thing I cared
about.

Once acceptably tamed and submissive, however, I'd lost my fire;
no suitable option at that point but set me to work on the street
like the other ones.

Now, here he was again... standing right in front of me.

His cool, languid gaze still belied the canny shrewdness that
could see directly into anyone. He deciphered me in the same exact
way as always, and I knew he had immediately and accurately assessed
the entire situation.

In an appealing gesture, he extended his broad palm toward Jenny
and said **Hey— my name's David. How you doin' today?**

Jenny was utterly speechless — totally blown away by this potent
concentration of 'man-ness'.... a physical force I am sure she had
never before encountered in her entire sheltered little life.

What the fuck was he doing *here*?? I felt an imperative to get
Jenny away from him as soon as I could. His magnetic charm and
virility were SO ensnaring; I was scared for her....*and* me.

May I? he asked, and moved to sit beside me on the bench.

Stammeringly, I introduced him to Jenny *myself*, making sure to
call her "my girlfriend". He again extended his huge hand to her
and when she took it, kissed hers, then flashed that killer smile
once more.

Maybe it was fever, but I could have sworn I saw tiny rainbows dancing in his dense, softly-glowing afro and the glossy moustache and sexy beard that set off his perfect chocolate lips. His skin's the color of rich Kona, and every bit as smooth — and the rounded musculature of his he-man chest and strong arms was evident, even though his brightly colored shirt had long sleeves. I felt hot — and realized I was starting to swoon. With the flat of my hand, I gracelessly wiped the gathering dampness from my forehead and neck.

So, what brings you HERE? I asked, after rasping an explanation to Jenny that he was an old friend of mine from San Francisco.

My sis died he answered, and told us he would only be around a few days. He was in town for her funeral tomorrow, he said, and had just dropped by the park to check out whether or not anything interesting might be shaking there. He was not familiar with this particular part of the country (much less, this city) but had surmised that an urban park was usually a happening scene, if one was searching for some action.

Me and Lute here, we dig our trouble he winked. **Don't we, Lute...**

My head was swimming. I *was* feverish, and a quiet panic was beginning to take hold of me as I thought about all the questions Jenny would surely put to me tomorrow, and about how I'd manage to stay out of bed with David <u>tonight</u> (that is, if he even *wanted* me, for his keen attention seemed to be riveted dangerously on HER). **Fresh meat** I thought; I *had* to get us away from him.

She at last found her voice and said **I'm so sorry about your sister! Was it sudden??? How <u>awful</u> for you!!!**

He placed that big palm over his heart, and dipped his head humbly. **Why, thank you** he responded, using his sincerest voice — its baronial tones outvying even the most sinuous cello solo... its deep vibration as penetrating as a sex toy.

Then, she said about the most distressing thing she could have; she told David about our plans to spend the day together tomorrow, and asked him if he'd like to drop by and hang out some with us — if the time and location of the funeral permitted it.

His answering "vibe" said: *"Aw shucks now ma'am, you flatter li'l ol' me"* but his smile was like a panther. I spoke up quickly, trying to hide the eyes-wide alarm her offer had triggered in me.

Jenny I said, *I was really hoping you and I might be able to— you know— just be ALONE together, tomorrow. No offense, David* I hastily added, *but you know how it is*.... Then, I winked, to match his earlier one. His counter-stroke was swift, catching me completely flat-footed.

Uh huh, yeah, I know; I can dig that, Lute. What you doin' TONIGHT, though?

Well, there it was....and I realized I wasn't sure what I truly wanted to say.

In order to effectuate a mishap-free tomorrow, all my faculties would need to be hitting their stride — however, every last scenario that might *possibly* go down if I chose to hang with David was certain to leave me depleted. Two constraints were squeezing as tight as my eros: not nearly enough time to clean up that mess before Jenny got there in the morning, and not having the place be smelling like spunk.

I made a rapid decision and spoke up again.

I'm going to bed early I said. **I want to be fresh tomorrow....
big day, you know....** and I gave another wink, for emphasis.

Ahhh, I hear ya, Lute. Gimme your number — maybe I'll give y'a call on Sunday.

Trapped.

At least, though, I'd survived *this* moment. I obediently wrote it down on my little notepad and handed over the slip of paper.

He craned his neck hard to see what was written on the top page — the one from the other night... the one with the license tag.

Uh uh I said as I closed the cover — shaking a warning finger at him and feigning coyness. **You not get see dis.**

Donning a sly smile, I returned the pad to my shirt pocket. I wasn't merely feverish now; my stomach churned with molten fire.

Uh huh, I gotcha, Lute, you devil. We'll have us a nice little talk on Sunday. It gets hotter the longer y'wait, y'know...

He addressed Jenny as he stood up.

So nice to meet you, miss Jenny. You take good care of my buddy here, okay? Lute's one of my favorites. He winked, and to further my horror, turned directly to me and purred **See ya Sunday, kitten.**

David took her hand and kissed it again, just like the gentleman he wasn't; he then nodded amicably to me and made his exit.

I was afraid I was actually going to hurl.

How could even <u>HE</u> say some rank shit like that in front of somebody's girlfriend??????

Jenny looked at me, and her mouth started to open.

Jenny, please — I stopped her with a firm wave of my hand. **Please. Not now. I'll tell you about it tomorrow, I swear.**

I told her that I really wasn't feeling well *at all*, and asked would she mind if I just laid back down again for a little while.

As I shuddered through anguished tremors, she cradled my head in her soft, welcoming lap, and I was so grateful for her — for her gentle, unquestioning acceptance, and her quiet empathy.

I wished I could weep, but even more, I wished willpower alone could just unhappen everything.

Saturday May 1

   Well, the big day had finally come, and even though I did manage
to dodge being up all night with David, I'd still barely slept a
wink. My miserable cold lingered, and of course, my nerves were
completely fried.

   Jenny arrived promptly at 9:30am....just like we'd planned.

   20½ North Welter Street has no entry system, so, I have to go
downstairs to wait for her — and as I sit there on the stoop,
Walter Brandt comes sauntering out. I've seen very little of him
since that night last November, when the things he had to say about
Hillary (my basement 'projection') had shattered my psyche. (He'd
later informed me, by the way, that she had been evicted, along
with her drug-dealing boyfriend.)

   Making sure my path crosses his as seldom as possible has been
my mission....(and is likely why he looked so surprised to see me).

   **Well look here — it's Jerome!! What's happening, old friend???
Where've you been....haven't seen you around much! Thought maybe
you'd moved out or something...**

   I mumble that I've been busy, been kind of minding my own
business... been dating. I add this last part, because I see Jenny
coming across the street, smiling at me and waving.

   She's clearly not wearing a bra today, and I'm wondering how
the hell she got away with it; there's no way in life her parents
let her leave the house like that.

   Upon introducing her to Walter Brandt and catching him ogling
her big, jutting breasts, I immediately excuse us and shepherd her
inside — because I'm about a ball hair away from knocking his
filthy teeth right down his lecherous old throat.

   Looks like a knotty day setting up here...

As if in perverse furtherance, I've already mixed us a pitcher
of stiff Bloody Mary's, despite that Jenny's not yet drinking-age.

I know she's booze-curious (along with the other 'curiosities'
natural for a girl of her age and inexperience) and I've decided a
couple of Mary's are no really big deal. Maybe they'll even put
her to sleep, and then (once the whole day has slipped by without
incident) I can wake her up when the protest is over, and she can
go home.

(I *myself* could certainly use a Mary....or two...or three; I
feel like absolute dog shit this morning.)

I sit her down at the kitchen table, and after placing one of
the ruddy cocktails before her, I take the facing seat and brace
for the barrage of questions.

Shall we toast? I ask, flourishing my glass in her direction.
To us I say, before she has a chance to reply.

The first thing she wants to know, is why David called me Lute.

This one's easy, and the explanation at least has some charm —
but then, she wants to know if *she* can call me that, too, since
she likes the sound of it, and loves its adorable story. She wants
badly to have a nickname for me, and of couse, I won't permit her
to call me Jerry.

I know how painful it will be for me to keep hearing that name.
It will keep carrying me back to San Francisco and feed even more
distress into my ongoing struggle with my complexities. I ask
myself if it'll be worth it, if this might make me have to confront
these things head on (instead of constantly skirting their horrors
as I keep [insisting upon] doing).

She's waiting for me to answer — watching my face, and trying
to figure out what in the devil is going on behind it.

Of course, you can— I say (although I have not decided) **—if you
dig it.**

I wish she wouldn't keep forcing me to make choices I'm not yet ready to make. What the fuck is *that* all about*??* Her little pill might be sweet, but its bitter aftertaste will curl your damn toes.

My turn now, so, I ask where is her bra.

Slipped it off during the bus ride down into town, she giggles. Just unhooked it through her [über-thin] t-shirt, stealthily pulled the straps through her sleeves, and voilà! It's not considered very cool these days to wear a bra, but I know her parents make her, because we've discussed it. It doesn't surprise me that she'd take this opportunity to go without one, what surprises me is that she's so *comfortable* going without it... which both impresses and arouses me. Plus, her opulent tits with their fat, eager nipples are one-hundred-percent <u>fantastic</u>.

It is *definitely* going to be a knotty day here.

Okay, so now she wants to know who David is, and how I know him. I can feel myself going red from fingertips to scalp, and my eyes lose focus. I'm trying to remember how I had planned to answer this, but last night was such a sleepless wallow, all the ribbons of thought spinning around in my head got tangled together, and now, the separate streamers are just one giant ball of colored bits — with no ends sticking out to grab....and no labels.

Uh, we were just friends I manage, my mouth buzzing. **We knew a lot of the same people, and everybody always ran into one another during...you know...protest marches, and happenings, and shit like that. Our crowds kind of overlapped... sort of.**

I'm starting to think maybe my best bet *is* to just take her to bed. We won't have to talk so much then, and I know a lot of fun games I can teach her. We could stay there all day, and our dialogue would be able to evolve more naturally. Yep, I'm starting to think laying her down might not be a bad idea at all...

That's IT?? That's __all__ you've got to SAY about that guy?!?

Jenny's a bright girl, and she knows there is a LOT more weight
to this story than the fluff I have just tried to peddle her. I
turn yesterday's incident over and over, reliving every minute she
surely is, too; it is undeniable that there's SO much more to
whatever was (is??) between David and me, than these rank fragments
of bullshit I'm selling.

As her irritably arched eyebrows and rising color project ALL
of her perceptive skepticism, a brutal edge she's not shown me
before, shows up with a racy scintillance — and as if things
aren't already precarious enough, her pungent impatience with me
feels kinky... and right away, my cock is locked in its fist.

NONE of this is good, so, I make the only move I can.... and
that's my vicious, unadorned candor.

Wipe that look off your fucking face, you goddamned pricktease
I snarl. *Like you don't have ANY idea how BAD I want you..... You
keep rubbing all over my thighs, and it makes me __NUTS__ — then, you
decide you oughta kiss me, too, just to shove some __MORE__ shit in my
mug..... and you HAD to know what those big-ass knockers of yours
were gonna DO to me — how MUCH do you think I can __TAKE__, Jenny?!?!?*
CUT ME SOME MOTHERFUCKING SLACK, ALREADY!!!!

She stands up slowly; I'm wondering if she's going to throw her
drink in my face, or slap me, or start to cry... or just go away
and finally allow me peace. She strides over and pulls my head
between those remarkable breasts, pressing that soft, sexy body
hard against my torso.

Oh, I wanted her... we spent the *entire* day in my bed.

This horrible morning, every thought is about the wicked thing I did yesterday, and all I want to do right now is die in this bed I haven't even the strength to leave, and make it a shallow grave.

I cannot *believe* I stole Jenny's virginity, and I cannot imagine how I am going to live with myself for doing it. I toss and turn endlessly, but the torment doesn't let up. How could even *I* commit such an irremissible sin???? I should not be allowed to live.

That I 'protected' her so carefully was baser still, because all of that BS I'd sold myself about the 'pure' sort of experience that should be Jenny's first time, was vilely disingenuous. I'd mused that she deserved 'someone better, and much more committed', when 'committed, <u>PERIOD</u>' is the real sentiment I was ducking.

NOT protecting her would've actually been more *decent* — since if things went awry, we'd at least be in it *together*... for "better or worse", like Ms. T always touts. But now, I can just walk away like nothing ever happened — no evidence of me left there at all (except the ugly, unnecessary scar I have left on her future).

Because I WILL walk away... and I know it.

Peril's Park hovers deep within the black havoc. A heroin death would bring me duly full-circle, but it *has* to be that drug, thus, I *cannot* risk a shiv, and the unworkable bind snowballs into chaotic desperation....until I suddenly remember David's supposed to call, and at last, I find the solution.

We could go together, as soon as it's dark — for not a soul over there would dare even *dream* of rolling a force like *HIM*. We could safely score, come back here and fire up, and then, he can fuck my damn brains out. Once he falls asleep, I will cook myself a *lethal* fix, and get the hell out of here for good.

It's a perfect plan, and I like it. There is nothing to do but wait for that call... and yet, my head keeps right on grinding. It grinds, but I can no longer think straight — and since my efforts leave me all the more frantic, I wish I could just rip out my mind, and throw it right through the goddamned window.

I shut my eyes and hide beneath the sheets, as if that might help me vanish... but it doesn't.

Instead, behind those closed lids, I find Floyd.

I see him walking back and forth, back and forth, and I discover he's not behind my eyelids at all — it's my heart's eye that is watching him. I could be blind, I could be dead, and I know I'd still see him.

Why didn't I just endure Jenny's questions*???* Why was I willing to end up like this, just to keep from confronting a past I have learned I cannot outrun*???* (David showing up is proof I can't, if ever there *was* any.)

If only I had been able to stand in my space and *take it*, Saturday would be all over with and wrapped up neatly; I'd be strolling over to 2016, looking for my beloved.....

However, if only I had been able to <u>STAND IN MY SPACE</u>, I would have never lost my beloved in the *first* place. I keep fucking up and taking everyone else down with me; it HAS to stop.

Thinking of (Seeing*?? Feeling???*) Floyd, has strangely grounded me. I begin to realize I *don't* want David to fuck my brains out, and I *don't* want a deadly O.D. I don't want to have to face Jenny either, and mangle her heart when I explain how I've sinned against her... but I will, because I know I must own it. I have to stop running, because running has *clearly* cost me the very thing that I treasure the most.

Even so, I am way too weak and sick this Sunday, to get up and go searching again; I'm just too devitalized to handle it.

I keep getting this sense of Floyd's "nearness"— like I'm about to run across him — but today it just would not end well. I don't want to go *anywhere*, because I'm so afraid I'll see him disappearing around a corner (or something far worse), and I'll have a blackout in public, and they'll want to put me away again.

93

It's not worth the risk; I can't afford to waste my chance to tell him how I feel — how I have felt all these long, wretched months... and I might only get one shot at it.

The best option (the *only* option) is to just stay put... and figure out a way to bear myself.

I will rest today, that I might make it to work in the morning, and I will come up with a plan for how to proceed with Jenny when I see her there. Who knows — perhaps she'll have caught my cold (we sure swapped enough fluids to accomplish *that*, for shit's sake) and her parents will make her stay home until she's better.

If not that, well then, tomorrow I must accept the thrashing I deserve — and what I deserve, should flay the flesh right off my good-for-nothing bones.

That's still okay. I will simply gather up the remaining mess and go lay it down at Floyd's feet.

When the phone finally rings, I don't answer.

As the little car scooted along the city's streets, even the most committed of pedestrians ventured covetous glances.

It might be spotted almost anywhere around town, but it was usually near an upscale restaurant or club… or on the street it lived. Its carmine brilliance always made it seem like a nimble, vivid bird darting amidst a flock of drab, clumsy others. This was Chad's baby — custom, sharp, noticeable; here, and then gone in a flit.

He loved having his hands on the steering wheel… loved being in masterful control.

He liked nice things, and he liked being noticed for nice things. He liked going to nice places, and hanging out with others who had nice things, too. He was not very attractive himself and neither were his closest friends (for none of them enjoyed *that* sort of competition). They liked keeping a few beauties around, though, because they were so savory to gaze at and to paw.

Floyd was ideal for this, with his princely looks and charming manners… and those *eyes*. Chad liked glancing over at him from behind the wheel— liked watching the wind lifting that satiny black hair, as the warm-toffee skin drank the sun. At times, Chadwick could barely believe he could have something so fine as this, anytime he wished — and he treated it with singular care, to make sure that it stayed just as lovely as it was.

Floyd certainly did like to be pampered. His parents had doted on him and imbued him with that expectation.

Early on, they had chosen to educate their son privately (for their pockets were very deep, and they'd learned he was experiencing malicious bullying at his school).

They were outraged; this was a *posh* academy (where superior standards of behavior should definitely have been expected and [rightfully] demanded). It was because Floyd was queer and bi-racial, they were informed, and alas, nothing could be done. So fetching, though, and so impeccably courtly…. it was such a shame— it really was.

Immediately, they withdrew him, and they resolved to *never* put him through anything like it again. He was their little prince — a perfect little prince to spoil.

His clear ochre skin had been tended with loving care, and they'd robed it in the exquisite fashions he most enjoyed. He had his Nordic mother's silky-fine hair, yet it was a gleaming black, just like his Moorish father's. They decided not to cut it, allowing it to grow into the mirror-like, graceful waves that now brush his hipbones. They exposed him to fine dining and international languages.

The social shaming had already rent him, however, and the wound had festered unnoticed. It sat aching in Floyd's young psyche, and the pain of it drove him mad. He hated his parents — especially his genteel, dark-skinned father — for making him what he was, which was <u>BLACK</u>… because that is what they called him (although they used other words). They'd spit them constantly from their malevolent mouths and made him feel so filthy he'd run away sobbing. It was even worse than being called a sissy…which they also did (although they used other words).

His parents had pulled him out of school, but they hadn't realized that their great regret over having naïvely placed him there, would not be enough…that their loving and doting would not be enough. It had taken so long to even know the wound was there – and they were lost as to how to close it, once they'd at last discovered it.

Thus, out of ponderous guilt, they accepted his contempt for them, and did everything they could to try to make up for something they could not: the fact that they were profoundly in love and wanted nothing more than to be together. Their treasured progeny was to be the most precious gem in the crown of their marriage, but it had just not turned out that way.

When at only nineteen, Floyd became irrevocably smitten with Carmen, they'd been understandably dismayed. Not only was she three years older, she was a divorcée with a child by another man. They'd surmised the homosexual proclivity of their son, but he was still budding; his blood was hot….and so was <u>Carmen</u>.

His parents ached for him, because they feared the relationship could not endure once his authentic nature eventually emerged.

Floyd wouldn't hear <u>any</u> of it. He and Carmen were *made* for each other, he insisted. They looked so convincingly good together, it almost seemed as though she completed him — and yet, it turned out she merely reflected him; what he saw in her was his own Venus.

The odds were against them, and everyone knew it but Floyd and Carmen (who thought she'd found in *him* the debonair, devoted mate she'd long sought. He even loved her young daughter, who had adored him instantly). The couple took the child and ran off to wed — the coup de grâce to his parents' hearts — for it was clear, then, they had lost him, and that his hatred would never stop.

They acknowledged they must give up… and, their sorrow joining them closer still, they turned away. He never even knew he had been abandoned.

Floyd wasn't particularly fond of Chad's 'baby'. He did like the color and the cleverness of its sassy profile (so visually high yet so physically low, at once). The problem was that (despite its deluxe interior) the car was simply not comfortable for him. He was really just too tall for it, and couldn't ever seem to get quite situated – but he knew how much it meant to Chadwick, and chose to never complain.

For *this* Sunday's ride, they'd been zipping around in the exhilarating fresh air way out on the compass of the city. The sky was an endless celeste dome, and the beguiling, tangy whiffs of floral perfumes wafted everywhere. The bright springtime was veritably ringing with intoxicating charm.

Chad marveled at how such wide-open spaces brought his lover so sensuously alive. Floyd had a reserved polish (even when he donned the blithe persona of his socially entertaining performances), but out in nature he transmuted — becoming an indecipherable creature that was arcanely unearthly in its comsummate earthiness. Unnervingly wild and mystic, it danced enticingly – always just out of reach.

Venturing off the road, they walked along a little brook that ran beside a shaded grove. Chadwick had been so stirred by his magical treasure, he'd led Floyd into the shadows and enjoyed him against a tree — finding it nothing short of transcendental to experience him thus.

Now, however, they were tooling around back in town, and the car cruised along the busy artery that divided Peril's Park.

The younger man contemplated the park as they passed. Of course, it wasn't really called Peril's Park… Jerome had named it that.

They'd split their sides one day, as he'd been mimicking for Floyd, the assorted characters that hung out there overnight in their edgy, precarious culture. Amigo seemed to know all about who and *how* they were —— he had their quirks, their walks, their faces, their unintelligible dialect, down to a riotous art. He'd dubbed the park perfectly; Floyd couldn't even remember its real name anymore.

Then, as if in response to this tacit musing, Chad made a few surprising turns, and the little car oozed down North Welter Street.

Why have you come this way? Floyd demanded. It certainly wasn't the usual route home.

I wanted you to remember what you got to leave behind, my love. I worry about losing you, Floyd, and thought perhaps I should remind you just how much I am willing to do for you.

Floyd gazed at Chadwick, slowly blinking his long lashes — a movement intended to hide the black rage in his eyes.

I will cut his throat while he sleeps he thought, and let a smile steal across his handsome face. It was satisfying just to imagine; of course, he would never do anything so stupid…or so gross.

In fact, his revenge *was* that Chad had turned down this street— because on this street, was the very reason Floyd would never belong to him.

Monday May 3

    Jenny indeed came down with my cold and didn't show up for work today. She'd ingested a considerable amount of my secretions last Saturday, and honestly, it would have been a miracle if she was able to resist so much exposure. I decided I would call and check on her when I got off; I felt guilty about having infected her, and guilty, too, about my relief at the reprieve from 'reckoning' that her illness had so conveniently bought me.

    My plan was to go straight home from work and wait until later to head over to 2016 (figuring that someone with that kind of bank probably wouldn't get home nearly as early as a basic wage-earner like me). I had no idea what I was going to do once I got there, but I knew I'd have enough time to come up with something... even after first giving Jenny sufficient telephone attention.

    As I walked in my door, though, the phone was already ringing.

    Damn, Jenny I thought angrily, *give me a fucking minute to at least catch my breath!*

    Despite my pique, I carefully composed myself between the moment I peevishly snatched up the receiver and the one I spoke into it my polite **Hello?**

    Heeyyy, kitten...where whuzzz you yesterday??

    I was dumbstruck. I had expected Jenny's voice congested with my germs, not David's velvet-cello croon. Spontaneously, and most unexpectedly, my eyes brimmed with scalding tears. I wanted to hang up, but I literally could not...and I could not seem to speak, either.

    He tells me how he tried all day yesterday, to reach me.

    (I guess he had; after a while, I'd turned the ringer off. The strident sound of its jangling insistence had begun to jeopardize the delicate equilibrium I'd managed to establish, and I just couldn't deal with it anymore.)

He wants to see me, to hang out with me, and catch up on lost time. He tells me he scored a little treat for us the other night and wants to turn me on to it. He wants to know where I live. He says how much he's missed that sweet tail of mine.... and that freakish loving I always gave him.

The whole time he keeps calling me Lute — Lute this, Lute that, and it slides around in his melodic phrasing and loiters in the hypnotic vibration of his voice.

(I imagine that this is what it sounds like when the devil calls for you. You know you're about to burn alive, and that it's going to hurt like — well — <u>HELL</u>..... but you go anyway.)

Ms. T would have a major stroke if she had any idea I was listening to David. (For that matter, so would my parole officer.)

I know I must not give in — not because Ms. T has managed to rearrange me or because Mr. P will threaten me, but because I've realized I don't want to live in hell with David anymore. He knows all he can get from me, but right now, he'll settle for just a little piece of it; when he can get more, he will take that too.

I still have not spoken — there is just so much that's pressing to get out all at once... but as my brimming tears breach, my brain and my guts and my heart finally meet at my mouth.

Where were you when they locked me up?!? I yell through the gasping sobs I cannot control. **_Where were you when they put me away??? You don't care about me, you NEVER cared about me!! Stay the fuck away from me! STAY THE FUCK AWAY FROM ME!!!_ <u>STAY THE FUCK AWAY FROM ME</u>_!!!_**

I've lost it; I'm hysterical. I'm glad he's not here with me, because he'd just smother me in his imposing arms and shush me with caresses and kisses and his sing-song voice. He'd crush me against his unyielding body and take advantage of my desperation, hone in on my debilitating weaknesses....and then, exploit them. He might even stick a needle in me.

NO NO NO!!! I'm shouting, and I grab the phone and hurl it against the wall, as out-of-control howls come ripping out of me. They leave me without the strength to stand, and I see the floor approaching.

I must have blacked out; I don't know for how long, but it was dark when I woke up. I suppose this is why they used to resort to just strapping me down and leaving me to lie there.

I do feel better now, though... unfucked and safe, with no new marks on me.

Looks like I'm going to need a new phone.

Chadwick was beginning to stew.

The outing earlier today had been exceptional, and most of this Sunday evening he'd spent as planned: zealously preparing for an eagerly anticipated business trip…. but now, those high spirits were in danger of deflation.

The week's meetings were being held in Las Vegas, and a whirl of anticipation had Chad swept up, as he looked forward to some high-stakes gambling (and some lively good-timing, too) with his handsome companion at his side.

That companion, though, was still sitting in the huge living room… just sitting there, pensive and quiet. He'd made no move to get up and start packing.

Floyd was *always* assiduous about travel preparations, for everything had to be just right —— just the right wardrobe for dining, for clubbing, for lounging. He was not the type to hastily throw something into a bag and go; his planning was admirably careful… *always*.

Their flight left early tomorrow; why wasn't he getting ready*???*

Chadwick decided to take his agitation straight into the living room. He also decided to start with just a casual air — a simple, innocent inquiry which he hoped would mask his heightening stress.

Don't you think it's time you started packing, my love? I don't want you to be tired in the morning. At this rate, you're going to be up all night.

Standing behind the plush sectional where Floyd sat so meditatively, Chad reached down and adoringly stroked the stately head — its hair as black as obsidian and equally reflective.

I think I will not go with you this time Floyd answered. ***I don't like Las Vegas; it's cheap and it's vulgar.***

Chadwick was flabbergasted. Never before had his pet defied him. He must not have heard correctly.

What do you mean, you think you won't go? Of course, you will go; I want you to. It'll be fun — just think of it!

Chad realized his words were not landing the persuasive 'punch' he'd intended. Floyd should have turned to him and said he was only teasing, only wanting to see whether he could get a rise out of him. He should have gotten up with a charming smile and said he was just waiting to see how long it took before Chad came and paid attention to him, and that he'd planned to begin packing the moment that happened. Maybe he would even laugh and then grab Chad playfully — just to mess with him further, and [ideally] get him horny.

Floyd did not smile or laugh, nor did he rise.

I don't want to go to Las Vegas he said. *I want to stay home.*

This was too much for Chad. There was no way he was leaving Floyd at home, *especially* considering how strangely he'd been acting lately. His body had seemed tense — not compliant and yielding like Chad was accustomed to — and his eerie green eyes always seemed to be focused on something Chadwick could not see. He'd never felt truly comfortable trusting Floyd, and now, he was near panic as it became undeniable that his prize was clearly distancing himself.

You will NOT stay at home, Floyd, you will come with me. I told you I want you to, and I should not have to say it again. Please come and pack — I don't want to be cross with you.

When Floyd got up and faced him from the other side of the couch, Chad was struck for the first time ever, that his lover's youth, vigor, and statuesque frame were not traits to merely salivate over —— they also made him a formidable physical opponent against whom Chad was at a distinct disadvantage. He'd fight him, though, if it came to that — and he glanced covertly around for something he might be able to use as a weapon. For his own equalizer, Floyd chose words.

Why can you never respect my needs, Chadwick? Why must everything always and only be about <u>you</u>? I not only do not wish to go to Las Vegas, I <u>despise</u> Las Vegas. The thought of spending a whole week there, is more than I can bear.

Chad saw his opening and dove for it.

*Look, my love, it's not really a week. It's only five days, and if you like, I can maybe even skip the last one. I know you don't care for Vegas, but I love you so, and I've been looking forward to having you with me… otherwise, this trip would be torture. You put light into my life; I **NEED** you there.*

Floyd really *did* hate the place. They'd already been there several times since he moved in here, and the thought of having to go <u>again</u> depressed him profoundly.

He found the town repugnant, but was also finding it increasingly repugnant to tolerate Chad's somatic proximity. It had never been easy or fun, but to just "grin and bear it" had been worthwhile. He'd wanted for nothing… except now, he knew he wanted Amigo more than any of it.

This was madness; Amigo had clearly said 'no'.

Floyd hadn't even seen him in passing since that morning last November, when he'd closed his door on the youngster for what had turned out to be the final time. He'd never understood what went wrong, what he'd done to make Jerome turn away — but how *could* he, really, since he'd had almost *no* time to know him.

That they should meet at all was entirely unforseeable.

The old edifice on North Welter Street in which Floyd lived with his little family was far from sound-proof, and sometime in mid-November last year, they'd heard a male voice and the landlady's conversing in the hallway just outside of their unit. It sounded like a new tenant was renting the recently vacated one beside them, and they'd given it no more thought.

The following day, however (during his return from an early morning errand), Floyd caught a glimpse of Jerome leaving 20½ North Welter Street and heading off down the block. The building had only a dozen or so flats, and, as Floyd was familiar with pretty much every face living there, he assumed this unknown one must be the new tenant. Floyd's "way" with the other occupants (and pretty much everyone else) was his fluid, detached charm, but *this* sighting made him instantly crave <u>nearness</u>.

A magnetic 'puissance' that seemed to radiate from this person (draw *to* him??) was wholly enrapturing — but its atypical 'embodiment' rendered Floyd's captivity a perplexing mystery.

He was sort of tall-ish, but in no noteworthy way (in fact, he almost seemed 'scrawny'… and yet, the hot moxie he exuded was <u>inarguably</u> rough-and-tumble). There was that zany head of hair, too — a mop of blondish spirals that appeared to have seldom known a comb or brush. He looked *so* quirky – but oddly, Floyd found every trait irresistably adorable and endearing.

It made no sense whatsoever "on paper".

Still, the appeal was so potent he risked knocking on his new neighbor's door the next evening to 'borrow a cup of sugar'.

Suave Floyd: sheltered and spoiled; scrappy Jerome: street-smart and secretive. The pairing was about as unlikely as could be, and their fugitive time together was so fleeting — in entirety, no more than a few short weeks — but those few weeks were seared into psyche as if scored by a branding iron.

Floyd truly treasured his family – his young step-daughter perhaps the most – (although he ached for affinity with his four-year-old son, who despised *him* as he had despised his *own* sire). He'd yearned to retain Carmen's infatuation, but he was no longer able to pleasure her; thus, she had withdrawn it.

As an embodiment of a Venusian soul, when "love" fell apart, so did Floyd. The lavish pampering with which Chad had lured him, was not simply fabulous gifts; much more *essentially*, he provided the admiring affection that Carmen now denied.

Chadwick urged him to give up on her and move into the penthouse — vowing utter devotion and boundless indulgence if Floyd would just pledge himself and be faithful. A perverse wind, it almost seemed, had borne the strange boy next door then. Floyd lost his ardent heart to him, and when Amigo at last welcomed his body, the consummation had been mind-blowing.

Soul, body, and mind — Floyd was "all in" now and was determined to refuse this trip. With Chad away, he'd have enough 'space' to allow his love's enormity.

Maybe he'd call the young man — see if he could reason with him, could talk him into trying again. Might it have been one too many of his own racist rants? What then, if he confessed the malignant root… perhaps even sought Amigo's help in expunging it…?

He'd swear to never say anything disparaging again, to do whatever else it took to be forgiven and be back in those loving arms…

Come on, Floyd, and get ready — I mean it. I hate to be impatient with you, but you might as well know I will not leave you here without me.

Floyd wondered if maybe now *wasn't* the best time to make this stand, after all— if maybe he ought to make some arrangements for a softer landing before taking such drastic action.

He *would* telephone Jerome….while Chad was in one of his many meetings. He'd sound him out before ripping an irreparable hole in this cushioning featherbed.

It was sensible to first see if Amigo would even have him,.

This, he decided, was actually a much better course. They'd be out of town, where no prying eyes would be monitoring his movements.

You are right he smiled at last to Chadwick. **It will be better if I am with you. I can keep an eye on you then, and make sure that you do not cheat on me.**

Tuesday May 4

    Jenny was out sick again today, and I was dismayed by how much
I missed her. Our work 'stations' are not side by side, meaning
that on the job we really only see each other during breaks — but
the loneliness I felt knowing she wasn't at least somewhere nearby
suggested a dependence I found disconcerting.

    At lunchtime I hit the phone booth, anyhow.

    Her "hello" is whispered and gummy — delivered through a hoarse
throat and clogged sinuses — and I feel awful that I've done this
to her. She, however, is overjoyed to hear from me; she'd been
afraid I had "one-and-done" her, when I didn't telephone these past
few days... particularly since she hadn't even shown up at work.

    I apologize for not calling on Sunday (but don't offer why) and
explain that I couldn't when I got home from work *yesterday*, because
I accidentally broke my phone. I'd intended to rest a bit, then
venture out to a booth — but instead, had conked out in a long
nap.... and decided (upon awakening) it was too late to ring up,
for that might (to her parents) make me seem inconsiderate.

    My mouth is buzzing so hard, I'm certain she must be able to
hear it, but of course, she cannot. My account *is* partially true,
but I still feel mortified by how glibly I'm able to lie to her.
I am a heinous viper — and I DO NOT merit this lovely young woman
(who has done *nothing* to deserve the likes of <u>me</u>).

    I say I'm planning to buy a new phone — maybe as early as this
afternoon. It's not practical for me to go without one, I tell
her (although I know I almost never use it).

    I tell her also, that while *some* of my wipeout these past few
days had to do with the lingering cold we now share, much more of
it was that exceptional loving she'd laid on me Saturday (which is
the TRUTH). I can almost *see* her heart swell, and my self-loathing
gobbles this duplicitous success so greedily, it sickens me.

    Despite it, though, I continue.

Listen, Jenny I explain, *I __am__ going to see about getting a phone, but if I don't feel that great when I get off, I'll probably just go home and crash again.... and I might not get to call you back. You know it's not a good thing if I miss work, so, I need to look after myself.*

(I had told her a little about my probation — why it's so important I keep a steady job and put in a credible performance. Flattered I'd taken her into confidence, she'd vowed to support me in whatever cooperation I needed.)

However, I did <u>not</u> plan to crash.

I planned to go over to 2016 and lurk there until that red car appeared.... no matter *how* late it got. I really couldn't afford a new phone *anyway*, and I didn't mind not getting one until I knew just what number it was that I wanted to dial.

I arrived at the 2000 block around dusk.

There was no stealthy place to conceal myself, but on the corner of one of the cross streets was a tempered glass bus stop with a perfect vantage point. From the bench in there, the entire scene was visible; I could sit, and nothing (certainly not *THAT* vibrant little number) would be able to come or go, that I wasn't able to see.

I'd decided that once it parked, I would get up unconcernedly and mosey on down toward the next corner.... just like anyone else. If the driver was alone, I'd simply note the building they entered.

My course of action if Floyd was along, I hadn't yet determined, but I was prepared to wait, and planned to use the time productively to carefully figure it out. I'd brought my journal, and of course, my little scribble-notepad — so, I had plenty of stuff to keep me plenty occupied and busy.

The thing never showed.

Wednesday May 5

    Therapy day.

    Today, I don't know *what* the fuck I'm going to tell Ms. T.

    My emotions are in a spiraling nosedive, and since I sat out in
the night air for hours, my cold is back in spades. I'm utterly
exhausted, and my heart is shattered.

    I take my seat in front of her, and she doesn't even play the
waiting game — immediately, she says gently **What's wrong, Jerome?**

    Blindsided.

    I cannot remember a single tender or sympathetic moment from
her, and she blows into me like a bullet. I cannot speak, or I
will start to cry. She asks if it's okay if she hugs me, and I am
astonished to nod 'yes'.

    As she envelops me securely, I break down and bawl like a baby.

The good part (this Thursday morning when Floyd opened his eyes) was that Chad had honored his promise to leave for home today. The bad part was that Floyd had tried countless times to reach Jerome, to no avail.

The week had begun with the euphoric anticipation of hearing Amigo's "hello" and the chance to tell him how much he'd been missed and longed for. However, after days of persistent, unanswered calls, there was worry – and ultimately, despair.

Where could he be*???*

Floyd knew of Jerome's obsession with perfect attendance at his job, but he had no idea why this was. He assumed it was just another of his love's eccentricities, and he'd dismissed it as nothing more.

If he wasn't answering his phone, perhaps he was away — but if he was away, it'd mean he was missing work.

That would be very out of character, thus, maybe he *was* still going to work, but was spending his nights *with* someone… and the thought of <u>that</u> was unbearable. What if he was lying there incapacitated — what if he was even dead?!?

Floyd tossed and turned every night, trying to find a position wherein his heart might rest easier.

His distraction was demonstrable, so, he brushed aside Chad's interrogations with the credible excuse that the town was really getting to him – and he salved his patron with promises to try harder, and assurances that he reveled in the older man's company. He kissed and caressed, and disbursed false smiles like Halloween candy.

Now, they were finally about to go home, and Floyd could see if (at the very least) sleeping in a familiar bed helped… or maybe even, he could sneak a night's slumber on the balcony—— and get away again with the explanation that he'd been outside merely resting and had simply nodded off.

As usual, Chadwick was worried about whatever might be preoccupying Floyd so ceaselessly.

He worried, too, as usual, whether anyone had dared to fuck with his car while he had been away — and as usual, the cayenne-pepper baby was snoozing right there at the airport… in the parking lot where he'd left it for the week.

Often admired (as usual) but reverentially untouched, it waited to spring to life at his command.

Thursday May 6

   Ms. T (perhaps unwisely) did not press me to open up to her
yesterday afternoon. She said she'd had a cancellation for this
Friday and offered me that appointment instead.

   Her advice to me was: **Go home, have something healthy to eat,
and try to get some rest** — and I took it. I was just too physically
sick and entirely too 'heartsick' to spend another night out there
waiting for that car... when it once again might not ever show up.

   I went straight home, had a cup of chicken soup and some tea,
and was asleep in bed before dark.

   Today, I don't feel any sturdier, but mercifully, do feel less
neurotic — and it's most likely because I did get to skip therapy.
It looms like a huge, dispiriting hurdle smack in the middle of
every week.... and my life's strenuous steeplechase is more than
challenging enough without having to add that particular obstacle.

   It might be different if I felt Ms. T was assisting me, but she
only wants to take me apart and remove the elements she doesn't
get or like. I will no longer allow this dismantling; all I truly
want and/or need from her are a few specialized skills to help keep
me from skidding right off the damn track. (I've wondered if I'm
not just 'skidding off' again now, in the kind of tailspin that's
so typical of me.)

   Speaking of 'hurdles', Jenny's out again — but today, I'm glad
of it. Nevertheless, I phone during my lunch break and learn she
will just take the rest of the week off, and come back in on Monday.
Good news for me, since I want to add nothing more to my plate;
it's already about as full as I can manage.

   Obviously, I need to clean it off.

Might I have blown this 'Floyd thing' way out of proportion...?

Maybe it's simply that I can't have it; maybe that's what's got me looping. There were only those few short weeks of "us".... is it even possible for this "Big Love" (like I *think* I'm feeling) to arise that quickly? (Particularly since its intimate consummation was so unbelievably transitory??)

I've tried convincing myself that the whole fixation is just a predictable rerun of my obsessive nature and demented libido, but my heart forbids the lie.

Well, tomorrow's payday; on Saturday, I will buy a new phone. If I can get smart and get back 'on track', perhaps I'll have the number I'm seeking, before the end of next week.

It was almost impossible to believe: Chad said he'd be going to his office tomorrow.

Floyd had been certain Chad would take Friday off and enjoy a long weekend (especially having lost part of the Vegas stay, to honor that vow to cut the trip short and come home prematurely). Not only had he said he'd be going in, though, he was planning to do it early, because rush hour traffic was ***"always such a fucking* BEAR *on Fridays"*** and he wanted to beat it home.

He'd also encouraged Floyd to go out "shopping or something" while he was gone all day, because Chad really did feel a little guilty now, about dragging him to Las Vegas. He knew how much his lover despised it, and so, how very much it had cost him to participate——and to be nice about it, as well, because Floyd could be a royal bitch when he wanted to.

Although he *had* kicked up that fuss about having to go, his behavior while there had been so charming and courageous, Chad felt a compelling urge to reward him.

During this last trip, Floyd had seemed *so* shaken that Chad actually wondered if he <u>should</u> be allowed to abstain (at least occasionally) from these frequent Vegas junkets. Daytimes in the tacky town were deathly dull for Floyd, and the nightlife Chadwick adored, the younger man found coarse and lurid.

It was just that Floyd had been acting so 'off' lately; Chad was genuinely concerned that he might be on the move, and couldn't bring himself to leave his pet at home alone and unsupervised. As always, however, he was forced to admit there were really no *obvious* cracks in Floyd's slick veneer, other than that weird edginess he seemed to be having such a hard time disguising.

What could be so secret, other than another lover?? Chad was still loath to trust him, but Floyd had been so sweet and patient, he'd earned a little time off the leash to stretch his long legs, and get some fresh air. Besides, Chad knew that since Floyd could not guess what time his benefactor might get back home, he wouldn't dare be away for too long.

Once they'd returned from Las Vegas, Floyd managed to snag a private moment to place another covert call to Jerome's number, but still, there was no answer.

He wished he hadn't taken so long to acknowledge the truth of his passion and that he hadn't been more determined to fight for it. He wished he had started trying to reach Amigo long before now.

Then, he remembered again that Amigo had said "no", and he wished instead that he could just go back to shouldering the whole sorry mess aside and try to enjoy this plush featherbed, since he'd managed not to rip it.

Friday May 7

     Shit!!!

     When I woke up this morning and checked the clock, I discovered
I'd overslept... *A LOT*. My first impulse was to grab the phone
and let my boss know I'd be in just as soon as I could get dressed
— but then, I remembered I had no phone, and I one-hundred-percent
freaked.

     My boss is absolutely livid with me, because I've not only made
Jenny sick, I've managed to infect another coworker, also — which
means he's down not just one, but *two* employees on the tiny staff
he already keeps so woefully inadequate. He doesn't like me, but
as long as I don't fuck up, he's really kind of stuck with me —
and now, I'd fucked up.

     I skipped bathing altogether — just dove into some clothes and
dashed for the door, figuring to give him a call at the very first
phone booth I got to. I raced down the stairwell and sprinted the
vestibule, and as I banged through the front door of the building,
Floyd rose from the stoop and turned to face me.

     All perspective vanished.

     The whole world blanked when I sprang into his arms, and the
collision spun us giddily around. As our mouths met, I tasted the
unforgettable essence of him — and that familiar, untamed effusion
permeating my every sense, was as dizzying as any drug.

     He grabbed a fistful of my hair — tilting my head to search my
eyes... finding the same as I saw in his. In that still morning,
we clung together like we didn't dare let go again.

     Mi Amigo— he breathes at last into my ear, **mi amor, how I have
missed you!!** and when I'm finally able to form a cohesive thought,
it's to wonder how in the world I've managed to endure existing
without him.

There is no way in life I'm going to work now; I am taking him home with me, and we are raunching until the cows come home.

Floyd tells me that we should probably not be seen out on the street this way — that his lover is jealous and suspicious, and that he doesn't want to risk having eyes on us. We go upstairs, we're kissing and kissing; it won't take but a few minutes for me to go back down to the phone booth and call in sick to work.

The first thing my boss did was swear at me; then, he fired me.

I didn't care. I didn't care about that. I didn't care about Jenny, I didn't care about Ms. T or my appointment *with* her this afternoon; I didn't care about my check-in with Mr. P early next week. All that I cared about was laying Floyd down on my bed and making love with him all damn day long.

He was already there waiting for me — naked and sinuous, caramel and licorice... and every bit as hungry as I.

As we snuggle together in dulcet afterglow, the sun sends warm, honeyed shafts through the window — the same window from which I'd watched the snow so many months ago....the snow that fell so steadily, burying our love beneath its cold, silent blanket.

We begin to talk.

Floyd tells me how penetrating a sense of my presence has been, how he hasn't been able to rest or focus anymore. He tells me how he has tried all week to reach me, how desperate he had become when he could not — and I lie that I'd tripped over the phone cord, and that the machine broke apart when it hit the floor.

I *do* tell him about the pharmacy, though, and confess I've been stalking the red car. I tell him about deciding upon "2016", and he confirms with great astonishment, that it is indeed the address of his posh prison.

He explains the dynamics of his relationship with the man he calls "Chadwick" — how suspicious Chad has been lately, and how Floyd's been increasingly unable to allay this growing distrust. Although he doesn't believe it's yet the case, he does not imagine Chadwick to be above even having him tailed. He wants to leave him outright, he says, and come make a life with me.

This is suddenly sobering; how can I even *hope* to support a lover like this — one accustomed to having <u>everything</u> — when I don't so much as have a *job* anymore??

Floyd, I just got fired is my next confession.

I will work he then offers gallantly. **I have worked before.... I was not successful at it, but for you, Amigo, for <u>US</u> — I will try my best.**

Its sincerity stirs me, but the idea is nuts. Floyd's clearly not built to hold down a job.

He is kept and coddled (even Carmen spoiled him), and although I know nothing about his life growing up, I'd bet big that his parents pampered him, too. His innate appetite for indulgence would very soon starve, for the only lifestyle I can offer is just entirely too lean. We'd be at each other's throats in no time.

I tell him that at least for now, we must let things lie, and fly low, under the radar. He should do all he can to not tip our hand to Chad, and I will hustle like hell to find a new job.

(I suppose I could even try pleading with my boss to give me another chance. His staff is miniscule, after all, and while he loathes me, he knows he can pretty much count on me to show up — even when I'm sick as a dog, and the others fail him.

This thought, though, brings Jenny to mind. If I don't go back there, it'll be easier for me to simply disappear, and I won't have to face her every day. Because it's got to be over with her; Floyd has returned to my side.)

Pondering Jenny, I remember (in a panic) the malevolent cold I've quite likely just spread to Floyd. Frantically distressed to have compromised him, I lay out how treacherously contagious I've been.

He gives me a tantalizing, marathon kiss, and says he'd be proud to have my cold — which excites me, and I want him again. However, he gently restrains me... telling me he needs time now to bathe and rinse the smell of our sex out of his hair. He should not risk the scent of a strange shampoo, he explains, and his long hair takes a good while to dry. Even if he were to try hastening things with an implement (which I don't have, anyway) the texture will change, and Chad will wonder at it.

My eros will not subside, so, I beg to keep holding him close. I ask when I can see him again, but he tells me he isn't sure.

He adds, though, that since he now knows my heart, his serenity is restored... which will prove an immediate boon. Chad, he assures me, will be thrilled to see the eerie preoccupation vanish, because constantly finding Floyd sitting so rapt and still as he endeavors to decipher my urgent telepathy, has been making the man altogether desperate.

Keeping Chad happy (and in the dark) will become his full-time job, he then tells me — suggesting that if he performs credibly, he will begin to earn more trust, and by extension, more freedom to move about unattended.... which of course, means more of me. It's even possible he might be able to funnel some monetary perks our way.

Well now I think, *here is a mind that is clearly as artful as my own...* and I begin to realize how little I actually know him. I'm starting to wonder if he has ever been as cagy with *me*, as I have (at times) been with *him*. If so, I am lusciously beyond my depth, for I know his perspicacity is even keener than mine, and I remember how easily he seemed able to read me.... almost from the very outset.

Despite knowing he possessed this rapier-like acuity, it had still never occurred to me that Floyd might be smart. I was content those few weeks, to just enjoy his blithe charm, his spellbinding looks, and ultimately, his addictive, filthy torridity.

Now, I can hardly wait to delve his psychology — which is, apparently, much more complex than I'd ever imagined, and which (I'm beginning to realize) is likely to ensnare me inescapably.

When can I see you? I continue to press him. *How soon can you get away again?*

Please, Amigo. I really need to bathe now. We can talk more as my hair dries. He kisses me, slips out of my embrace, and turns to head for the john.

This building is too dated to even have showers (Ms. L maintains it's because the old pipes aren't structured to provide the amount of water pressure that's needed). The bathrooms *do*, however, feature sumptuously deep clawfoot tubs... and they're large enough for <u>two</u>.

No, love he tenderly demurs, when I plug a little water play, *let me get on with this — it will allow us more time together in the future.*

As his hair dries, we strategize.

While he doesn't think he's as yet being followed, Floyd is totally worried about us being caught out together. Also, there are only narrow windows of time that present viable opportunities for him to come see me here, and unfortunately, these occur during the workshifts I'll most likely end up with.

That leaves the "happy hour" stretch of the day our best bet. Problem is, although it's customary for Chad to work deep into the evening, he likes cocktails and a late dinner at a tony restaurant afterward — and sometimes he wants Floyd to join him there, and Floyd must be available for that call. Occasionally, he just might come home for these, but Floyd seldom knows in advance.

Thus, even if we hook up the minute I'm off (assuming I *have* a job, that is), Floyd won't be able to get down and dirty with me here, clean himself up in time to conceal evidence of our tryst, and still be ready for Chadwick's whims.

It means that SEX for now, is out for us, leaving dating as our only option... and even *THAT* must be done with the utmost stealth. I try reminding myself: *"The longer you wait, the hotter it gets"* but the scorch is already blistering.

What meeting-place, though, might be safe for us? (Because if we meet here, we will definitely screw.)

Chad's friends *are* high-rollers, BUT, Floyd adds, since some of them fancy a 'common' treat now and then, it'd be *much* too risky for us to try hiding out at any of the familiar meat-markets around. Likewise, I sure don't want to risk running into Jenny in any of the joints I've frequented with *her*; with me not at work and without a phone, she will no doubt try checking for me in all of them.

I tell him I know just the spot, but he isn't going to like it. It's called The Cocoa Coast.

I explain that I went there a few times when I first got here from 'Frisco. I wouldn't say it's a dive bar, but it *IS* far from hoity, and its regulars are black homosexual men (retired seniors, primarily) who are decidedly "R&B" in speech, attire, and tastes. It's sparsely populated during happy hour, though, and there's no possible way Chad's asshole friends have *ANY* idea it's there — even if they <u>DO</u> fucking fancy 'slumming'. Its discrete location is also a bit further uptown....on a quiet little street well off the main thoroughfare.

(I *don't* say I'd gone in there back then, hoping to get my ass properly reamed..... and to see if I couldn't maybe even pick up a little side-cash in exchange for it.)

There's a jukebox that's stocked with old-school, sentimental love songs from the 50's and 60's, and sometimes a few of the men will get up and slow drag. Everyone is perfectly harmless, but they are clearly of African descent — and I know how Floyd feels about *that*.

I will try it he says, and I almost choke on my tea.

His face an embarrassed flush, he says he knows how repulsing is the ugliness of his racism — that in desiring so passionately to not displease <u>me</u>, he has gained a mortifying comprehension of the scope of his ghastly folly, PLUS a monstrous burden of regret.

Humbly, he asks my support as he seeks to escape the old bondage of his rage. He wants to open to me, to trust me with his 'keys'.

Perhaps this Cocoa Coast might be a good place to begin that, he offers; perhaps it was *meant* to be this way.

My emotions surge as a carnal heat. I pull him close, pressing hard against him, trying to thrust my hands inside his waistband... but he won't let me — and my ramping tension begins crowding out lucidity.

I can hear my own frustrated moans intensifying, as my agitation approaches its limits. Like a thwarted beast, I throw back my head in a foaming howl, but instead, **I love you!!!** is what cannons from my throat.

Saturday May 8

    This morning, the sheer gravity of my situation has hit me like
an anvil dropped from the sky. I have sacrificed my job (and maybe
even my liberty) just to steal a few fleeting hours with Floyd.

    He'd left my place in plenty of time for me to make my session
with Ms. T, but I was still lost in ecstasy, and equally lost as
to what I could *possibly* share with her — so, I skipped it. I
had already realized I was in deep, deep trouble, and not only did
I not want to sit down and face it, I most certainly did not want
to sort it through in front of *her*. Instead, I'd just gone out
and bought a phone.

    It's also occurred to me that I'll have to face Jenny *anyway*.
I can't afford to lose my final paycheck, and must go pick it up
at my workplace.

    I am, obviously, queasy as a billion dogs.

    While my stomach's always been edgy, things got way worse during
withdrawal; it's a whole-body trauma, but those abdominal cramps
are from HELL. They stole my sleep (and whatever weight heroin
hadn't already stripped from me). My volatile nervous system went
into hyperdrive, but I was too fucking sick to act up, (and hurting
too much, honestly, to even want to live).

    Ever since then, a racking nausea grips me when I'm really upset
(sometimes it's so bad, I can't keep food down). When I was little,
Grandmother soothed my jumpy gut with Chamomile tea; it still works
(which is why I drink so much of the shit).

    Thus, I've consumed it this entire distraught morning — and the
mound of sad, spent bags I've amassed, I have obsessively stacked
into a damp little cairn and dubbed "Pile of Worry Turds".... to
symbolize burying my stress beneath them. Panicking will sink me,
and although I'm frighteningly close to it, I *have* to keep it
together. As usual, I must reshape my self-inflicted debacle into
viable options; I must call forth rational mind and assess things,
that I might, then, craft a remedial course of action.

I start with what I've not as yet fully wrecked: my check-in with Mr. P early next week. I'll be in crazy-hot water with him for losing my stupid job, because I'm required to be employed.

It is alarmingly possible that if I fuck up, he just might want to <u>lock</u> me up, and I cannot let that happen — I cannot let him separate me from Floyd....and this brings me back to Jenny.

I did buy the phone; the very first thing I should probably do is head off the call she will no doubt place to me this morning (since I didn't ring up one single time yesterday) and tell her I've gotten a new one.

I'll explain that I was too sick to get out yesterday but won't let her know I got fired; she will receive that news from our boss himself when she returns to work on Monday.

(She will then advocate for me, pointing out to him the obvious dedication I've demonstrated by faithfully showing up despite my illness, and how he ought to recognize the uniquely dependable resource he has in me. She'll wonder why I didn't tell her I had been fired, but she'll wait patiently for me to explain why I chose not to.)

I know this is what she will do, because Jenny is so noble and well-intentioned, but today, I'm just not capable of coping with her. I plan to keep the conversation brief — explaining how depleting it was for me to crawl out (this morning) and get this damn phone (which I did <u>only</u> because trying to keep up with her via the booth on the street was sapping my already-enfeebled vitality). I will say that what I really need, is to just hang up now, please, and rest, and focus on trying to get better.

(I'll manage not to hate myself for these lies, because I'm in SO much trouble *everywhere*, I must first carve away little slices just to get to where I can wrap my hands around the real 'meat'.)

My tale will stir Jenny's heroic activist's heart, and she will leap to my defense... which *could* immensely help my cause (and I will manage not to hate myself for taking *this* advantage, because I know how much I need that job).

What I *can't* imagine managing, is encountering her every day at work. I just can't go on seeing her now that Floyd is back in my life....for not only will I be trying to be with him every minute that I have, he will occupy my entire headspace.

I've grown fond of Jenny despite my intention not to — but Floyd seems the very blood that runs through me, and there is no chance I can choose her. I've <u>no</u> idea how it's all going to go down, but I'm sure I am going to lose her.

These thoughts depress me, and the guilt of betraying her returns as such an awful weight in my heart, I decide that for now, I want [us both] to be assured that my affection for her abides... because it DOES. I won't have to lie about that, and I won't have to fake my feelings, because they are genuine (so genuine in fact, they are dangerous).

Next, I will try to reach Ms. T. Given my emotional collapse (and my no-show yesterday) she probably wonders if I'm dead.

On Wednesday, she shared her home phone number — an extremely rare act, as therapists are to maintain strict boundaries against this sort of intimacy. She was *really* concerned about me, though, and she busted through that rule like a frightened farm animal through a fence; I need to respect her compassion.

I can just imagine how worried she must have been when I didn't come in yesterday — especially since she'd failed to press me about what had me so upset (and knowing damn well that she should have). She has no idea my phone was broken, and likely tried to call... and of course, would've gotten no answer.

She'll certainly call my boss on Monday to see if I showed up
there, which would give me at least a couple of days to get my shit
(and my story) together.... except I know that as sure as the sun
comes up every morning, she will try again today, to reach me.

As with Jenny, I will call first, and head her off.

I will tell her that I lost my job; this is something I'm
obligated to do, and I dare not try to withhold it. I will explain,
however, that after Wednesday's meltdown, I'd overtaxed myself by
dutifully going to work on Thursday (even knowing full well I was
way too sick to be trying it). I was fucking wiped out, and simply
overslept on Friday.

I had also known I needed to act responsibly by immediately
replacing my phone (which, of course, got broken when I'd tripped
over the cord once I got home from therapy on Wednesday) but I felt
just too ill to stop off on Thursday and buy myself a new one.

Thus, when I woke up on Friday and found I was late, I panicked,
but when I went to call my boss and remembered I didn't even *have*
a phone — well then, I had *really* panicked. I will tell Ms. T that
as I raced around trying to get ready, I got more and more stressed
and started puking... and when I finally made it down to the booth
and called in to work, my boss just cussed me out and fired me.

I lie to keep surviving.

Grandmother is the only one I don't lie to, because with her,
I never doubt for a moment, my safety.

When Chad got home, Floyd had champagne cooling for him in a bucket of ice.

The minute he entered the broad foyer, he saw the younger man fairly floating toward him in pajamas of pale green silk—their unbuttoned top lifting back from his bare torso like a fluttering minty wave. Floyd smiled angelically, and kissed his lips.

Wow, what's THIS all about? Chad laughed, and through the gossamer fabric, let his hands savor the lean, tawny body.

I feel so much better, My Friend— I want to thank you for understanding, and letting me go out walking today. The fresh air revived me; it made me so happy, I just want to share it. I have chilled wine for you – let's go outside; we can watch the sun go down… and lay together.

Oh Floyd! Please don't say I "let you go out"! That sounds terrible — do you really feel that way?? I am not trying to make you a prisoner here! Do you REALLY feel that way???

His lover's words had indeed stunned Chad. He wondered now, if it *might* really feel like that to Floyd — especially the way he'd refused to let him stay at home and had dragged him to out to Vegas against his will. Maybe his own unrelenting grip was the *very* reason for the restlessness and distance he'd kept perceiving in his treasure. Maybe, he'd been crushing his lovely bird-in-the-hand to death!

But even so, everything was all right now. Floyd was smiling, and wanted to go outside with him, to enjoy the warm, late-day with him, to have <u>sex</u> with him. It was the kind of thing Chad lived for — and how very lucky he was, to hold this supple body so close, and to caress such exquisitely colored skin and such long, beautiful hair.

I understand that all you are trying to do is have me near you, My Friend. I am here because I want to be — but it IS better for me if I can get out by myself now and then; I like to walk alone sometimes… you know my legs are much longer than yours!

With that, he laughed believably – trailing his forefinger beneath Chad's chin, and playfully tweaking his chubby cheek.

Come out to the veranda, and lay with me on Tung.

Tung was the name Floyd had assigned the dreadful oversized lounger for two when Chadwick had it delivered. It was a curvy salmon pink chaise — much too inappropriately padded for its intended outdoor function — and immediately, Floyd had objected. He hated its garish and tasteless incongruity, likening it to a vulgar ultrasuede tongue. Chad loved it, though… it was perfect for snuggling, and large enough to get comfortably frisky upon. He liked its elbow room and its overstuffed support.

This was *beyond* outstanding! Floyd even had the wine bucket in swaddling wrap, already waiting. How wrong Chad had been to doubt him. All the younger man had really needed was to be understood — to have his profound spacial needs respected, and yes, <u>honored</u>. This would now be the case; Chad was determined to loosen Floyd's leash at least a little… as much as his unconscious need for control (and his rampant insecurities) would allow.

For *his* part, Floyd mirrored Chad's stroking and embraces, but heated himself with Jerome's memory: his wide, delicious mouth, his well-appointed privates, his redolence…

Chadwick pawed his lover's naked, compliant form from head to toe — yet he never saw the tiny passion mark hidden high along the ribcage— nestled discreetly just beneath Floyd's left scapula.

Monday May 10

    Jenny called today during her lunch break.

    Just as I'd expected, when our boss told her he had fired me
she went ballistic — reading him the riot act for not appreciating
my fealty, and then, swearing she'd walk if by the end of the day
he hadn't agreed to rehire me. She said he had visibly blanched
at *that* unexpected twist.

    Losing his two hardest working employees in rapid succession,
she said, he was obviously not willing to risk. He'd fume until
the very last second, but he <u>would</u> relent (she was *wholly* certain)
and grudgingly hire me back.

    I was immensely grateful to her, but *very* upset she had stuck
her neck out like that... and I told her so. She retorted that
she was a grown woman, and perfectly capable of deciding for herself
what sort of actions she might choose to take.

    (She <u>*is*</u> strong-willed, and unfortunately, that spicy defiance
really turns me on — which leaves me with <u>no</u> idea whatsoever, how
I will handle continuing to work alongside her. When I got fired,
the road ahead looked terrifyingly dark, but at least, I'd thought,
I'd be out of there... and the problem would be conveniently solved.

    Now though, I am traveling a *much* darker path, since it involves
the true affection I must admit I feel for her, <u>PLUS</u> my perilously
soft emotions. She wanted to drop by after work with an update,
but I said I was still sick and needed to stay away from her; I
said I wanted to unplug the phone and just rest.)

    A bit later on, Floyd called, too.

    Today...at 5 was the full extent of his truncated communiqué.

    I got to The Cocoa Coast about ten of.

129

When I entered the dim establishment, a few heads briefly turned
to ponder the white kid who'd chanced to stray in, but the bartender
recognized me at once, and waved. His name is Pres — well, Preston,
really. We'd tried a tumble all those months ago, when I'd first
arrived from the coast.

    Jerome! he hailed, grabbing my hand and shaking it with gusto.
How's it been, buddy?? Missed you around here!

    I explained that I had been trying to behave, had been working
to get my shit together and hadn't been going out to bars much
lately. I told him I had fallen in love and was there to meet up
with my baby.

    He called me a rascal, then, asked what I was drinking — and
when he'd made me the stiffest gin and tonic I'd ever tried to get
down, he leaned his elbows on the bar, and addressed me again.

    ***You look good, man. Managed to pick up a little weight.... I
like it. I like that hair, too.***

    Yeah I said, ***they want me to cut it, but—***

    DON'T he interrupted me curtly. ***Don't <u>do</u> that. It looks good;
don't you dare even <u>think</u> about it...***

    Pres had hated my hair from the jump; its mad obstinacy really
turned him off. In his opinion, it was bad enough to be white—
you ought to at least have nice hair.

    When I first met him, I'd finally emerged from what I call my
"institutional period", wherein the powers-that-be had determined
to cut off my long hair as part of normalizing me (that I might
look more like everyone else, and be more employable).

    My hair *doesn't*, though, lay down politely and surrender sweetly
to grooming. It defied them, despite all their doggedness, and
made me so miserable I refused to tend it. I'd *always* hated fooling
with my baffling corkscrews, but at least before they lopped them
off, a cursory rake-through from time to time with my fingers
sufficed. Pres just couldn't get with my hair (all the while
downright *swooning* over what he termed my "battleship" eyes).

We really weren't a bit well-suited, and with Ms. T doing her
dirty work, whatever we *had*, broke apart — but it all ended up
okay. Once I'd finally admitted that Pres fulfilled almost none
of my non-monetary needs, I realized I wasn't up to turning tricks
anymore (and it sure wasn't like I sent <u>HIM</u>, either). Everything
resolved perfectly fine, and our parting was mutually friendly.

This was the first time I'd been back since then, so, we got to
yakking about how business had been and gossiping about various
folks I remembered, when his voice trailed off and his eyes changed.
The bar's few other occupants paused also, and the room seemed to
fall strangely silent.

I swiveled my seat to face the direction they all were looking.

Floyd stood just inside the doorframe — his majestic, statuesque
handsomeness countervailed by a disarming shy vibe. He was dressed
very understated today: a plain pair of blue jeans clinging to
those sexy, narrow hips, and one of my old chambray work shirts
I'd given him quite early on and tried (in vain) to convince him
to wear.

Quickly, I hopped off my barstool and went over to greet him.
A close embrace allowed me feel how wildly his heart was racing
and to sense the tension steeling his long muscles.

In his strange, moss-hued eyes, though, I saw just loving trust.

Floyd I soothed, kissing him lightly, **come sit down with me,
and meet my friend, Preston.**

As we approached him, Pres extended his mahogany hand in a
genial greeting, and Floyd clasped it without hesitation. Nobody
else had gone back to minding their own business, however; their
riveted attention remained fixed.

He calmly introduced himself to Preston, and dealt.

I seem to have created a disturbance he said, (and it was true).
**I'm not really accustomed to bars, and I guess everyone can tell.
Or do I have toilet paper on my shoe, or something??**

Oh, don't worry about them Pres laughed. *We just don't see a lot of folks in here that look like you. I mean, are you a model, brother?*

Hey I piped up, glancing around the room with a grin, *eyes off my guy!*

The ice now broken, everyone gradually returns to their own conversations, but I still catch them sneaking a furtive peek from time to time. I'm sure they've all experienced their even share of handsome men, but not many, honestly, are as quite as striking as Floyd or share his unique exoticism.... so, I get it. Besides, that downbeat trip he's working today comes off hot as hell. The look exudes the machismo of someone <u>way</u> more than capable of defending themself — a side of him I'm totally unfamiliar with.

Its earthy, blasé brass implies that fucking with him might not be a great idea — and seeing it for the first time, I suddenly 'get' that Floyd's appreciable size has always been inconspicuous to me....a deception due to his slim shape, and guise of diminution.

There are so many things I don't know about him, and I'm aching now, to learn them all. He'd said he wanted to do this, to unlock 'Self' with me — but here at the bar (with so much riotous repartee, as Pres turns it up to "ten" to impress him), I can't see us getting a chance.

It would suck to end up back at the damn drawing board.

A selection is playing on the jukebox; it's a silky, feminine voice. The wistful lyrics are heartfelt and soulful... lilting through a slow cha-cha rhythm. She's singing about someone she'd lost long ago, but who apparently, has now returned.

"Seems like a mighty long time..."

As we smile at each other, I nod toward the tiny dance floor.